A shot whi
Ethan hun

"Anyone else you know ~~~~" Ethan asked.

"Could be anyone," she said.

"You can play innocent with me, but I don't think the marines are gonna be as warm and fuzzy."

"If you think you're warm and fuzzy," she said, yanking the car's back door handle, "then you're pretty clueless."

"We have to move. Shooter is going to change locations to get a better bead now that we're pinned down."

Kendra lugged Titus's dog carrier out, and Ethan reached in to help. Another shot pinged the metal car roof, sending off sparks.

* * *

Dana Mentink is a national bestselling author. She has been honored to win two Carol Awards, a HOLT Medallion and an RT Reviewers' Choice Best Book Award. She's authored more than thirty novels to date for Love Inspired Suspense and Harlequin Heartwarming. Dana loves feedback from her readers. Contact her at danamentink.com.

Books by Dana Mentink

Love Inspired Suspense

Military K-9 Unit

Top Secret Target

Gold Country Cowboys

Cowboy Christmas Guardian
Treacherous Trails

Pacific Coast Private Eyes

Dangerous Tidings
Seaside Secrets
Abducted
Dangerous Testimony

Rookie K-9 Unit

Seek and Find

Wings of Danger

Hazardous Homecoming
Secret Refuge

Visit the Author Profile page at Harlequin.com for more titles.

TOP SECRET TARGET

DANA MENTINK

HARLEQUIN® LOVE INSPIRED® SUSPENSE

Special thanks and acknowledgment are given to Dana Mentink for her contribution to the Military K-9 Unit miniseries.

LOVE INSPIRED BOOKS

Recycling programs for this product may not exist in your area.

ISBN-13: 978-1-335-49040-7

Top Secret Target

www.Harlequin.com

Printed in U.S.A.

There is therefore now no condemnation to them which are in Christ Jesus, who walk not after the flesh, but after the Spirit.
—Romans 8:1

To the men and women who serve bravely and selflessly,
and to the families left behind who do the same.

ONE

First Lieutenant Ethan Webb of the Air Force Military Police brushed past the startled aide standing in Colonel Masters's outer office at Baylor Marine Corps Base.

"The colonel is—"

"Waiting for me," Ethan snapped. "I know." Lieutenant Colonel Terence Masters, Ethan's former father-in-law, was always a step ahead of him, it seemed. Ethan and Jillian's divorce had cemented the bad feelings. He led Titus, his German shorthaired pointer, into the office, found Masters seated in his leather chair behind the gleaming wood desk. Mahogany, he'd been told, nineteenth century. Hard lines, unyielding contours and pretentious, like the man who owned it.

"You're late," Masters said. "And I don't want your dog in here."

"With respect, sir, the dog goes where I go and I don't appreciate you pressuring my commanding officer to get me to do this harebrained job during my leave. I said I would consider it, didn't I?"

Masters gave him a smug smile. "A little extra insurance to help you make up your mind, Webb."

Ethan glared. "It's a bad idea, like I said before. Leave me alone to do my investigation with the team at Canyon, and we'll catch Sullivan." They were working around the clock to put away the serial killer who was targeting his air force brothers and sisters as well as a few select others, including Ethan's ex-wife, marine naval aviator Lieutenant Jillian Masters. Boyd Sullivan was a killer with a flair for the dramatic, leaving a red rose as his grisly calling card, along with a note. "I'm coming for you." He had earned his nickname, the Red Rose Killer.

"*Your* team," Masters said with a nasty inflection on the first word, "hasn't gotten the job done and this lunatic has threatened my daughter. There have been sightings near our base indicating he's zeroing in on her. You're going to work for me privately, protect Jillian from Sullivan, draw him out and catch him, as we've discussed. We're playing offense here, rather than defense. It's a Marines thing, son. Maybe you airmen can't understand, but we like to face our enemies head-on." He steepled his fingers on the desktop.

Ethan fought to keep the anger from balling his hands into fists. Masters loved his games. Now he held the stick and Ethan was the bear about to be poked. "So you think I'm going to pretend to be married to Jillian again and that's going to put us in the perfect position to catch Sullivan? A couple of sitting ducks waiting to be shot?"

Masters stared at him. "You're going to prevent that, remember?"

He shoved a hand through his crew cut hair, striving for control. "This is lunacy. I can't believe you're willing to use your daughter as bait."

"I'm not," he said. "I've decided it's too risky for Jillian and that's why I hired this girl. This is Kendra Bell." He gestured to someone in the doorway.

The civilian woman stepped into the office and Ethan could only stare at her. That creamy skin, that curtain of red hair skimming her face... Shock ripped through him like rifle fire.

"You're..." He shook himself slightly and tried again. "I mean... You look like..."

"Your ex-wife," she finished. "I know. That's the point."

He swallowed hard and peered closer and the truth assembled itself as the surprise ebbed away. They did resemble each other, this woman and Jillian—same build, same eye color, same tint of hair.

She shot a distrustful look at Titus, and raised an eyebrow in Ethan's direction. "If you're finished staring...?"

He gulped. His mama would have boxed his ears to know he'd been ogling, but honestly, the resemblance was mind-blowing. Heat climbed up his neck.

"People used to mistake us for each other in high school," she said. "Sullivan's going to make the same error, and that's how I'll catch him, without your interference."

"My *interference*?"

She ignored him, turning to Masters. "You neglected to tell me, when I agreed to the job, about this scheme to involve Lieutenant Webb."

"I sent you a follow-up email," Masters said.

"Uh-huh." She folded her arms across her body. "Anything else you failed to mention, Colonel?"

Ethan tore his gaze away and locked eyes with Masters. "This wasn't part of the plan I heard, either."

"Yes, it was. I just didn't tell either one of you all of the pertinent facts."

Ethan blew out a breath and shook his head. "No way. Working with Jillian would be bad enough, but at least she's a marine, not a civilian, and she knows how to protect herself."

"So can I," Kendra said. "I'm a licensed PI, with a real gun and everything."

He cast her a doubtful look and started to answer, but Masters cut him off. "You will pretend to be newly reconciled husband and wife."

"No one will believe that," Ethan said.

"Yes, they will. I've already started the gossip wheels turning here and at Canyon that you two are an item. Posted an old picture of you two on a few key military networking sites."

Ethan gaped. "You…"

"And when Sullivan comes for Kendra thinking she is my daughter, you will catch him before any harm comes to Jillian."

"And what about the harm that might come to her?" Ethan snapped, jerking a thumb in the civilian's direction.

Kendra glared at him. "Don't talk about me like I'm not here. Like I said, I can take care of myself. Before I was a PI I worked as a bounty hunter, and there's plenty of excitement in that job, let me tell you. I don't need, or want, your help on this case."

His cheeks went hot again. "That's A-OK by me, because I'm not offering it. We're not working together. I'm out of here." He stalked to the door, his dog at his heels.

"Lieutenant," Masters bellowed. "You will not walk out on me."

Ethan turned and fired a glance at Masters. "I'm not one of your marines, Colonel, nor am I your son-in-law anymore, so with all due respect to your rank…" He let the slam of the door fill in the rest.

Kendra felt the crackle of energy leave the room along with Ethan Webb and his dog. She had recognized him from the file Colonel Masters had sent, but in person he was more impressive. The guy could be on a recruiting poster. Dark hair, eyes like coffee with a hint of cream, six feet of muscle and barely concealed annoyance, and a Southern drawl that thickened in proportion with his anger. His arrival had thrown her off her game. Time to get the meeting back under control.

Calm, cool and collected, she told herself. *Nothing you can't handle.* But it was hard to brush off the unsettling scene she'd just been part of, and more important, the text message she'd gotten that morning just before she'd dumped her cell and gotten herself a new number.

You're dead.

No further explanation needed. Andy, her ex-boyfriend, recently released from prison, where she'd sent him, had wasted no time starting up the threats. She'd escaped his sick world, but not for long.

Deal with that issue later, Kendra, she told herself. Sullivan was her target, and Ethan's abrupt departure was an advantage. Now she had the chance to try to persuade the colonel that she did not need any help catching the Red Rose Killer before he murdered anyone else in this part of Texas. Temporarily leaving her tiny office in Colorado, the place she'd fled after her disastrous time in Texas with Andy, the job was an answer to her prayer, the only way she could both settle her debt to Jillian Masters. She would complete the mission much easier without a second party in the picture, especially Jillian's ex.

She expected the colonel to be furious at Ethan's disrespect, but to her great surprise, he chuckled, leaning back in his chair.

"Hasn't changed a bit. He'll cool off and come around."

"How do you figure?"

"He's one of those Southern gentlemen types. Don't let his lazy Tennessee drawl fool you. He's smart as a fox and he's proud and hotheaded, but he can't walk away from a lady in distress."

"I'm not in distress."

"Not yet." The colonel smiled—a cold, calculating smile—like a tiger sizing up its prey. Her stomach tensed. She did not need another ruthlessly determined man in her life, but she had the feeling she'd just been saddled with two of them.

Ethan headed to the parking lot with Titus. He yanked open the truck door for the dog and got in himself, clenching the steering wheel, wondering how he'd lost control of his life. There was absolutely no reason he should be doing the bidding of his devious former father-in-law, and now to find out he'd be partnered with a civilian of all things. Why had he accepted the request that bordered on a command? Ethan was a member of the Air Force Military Police, not property of the Marine Corps.

Masters's previous words echoed in his mind. *Jillian needs you.*

That was rich. His ex-wife didn't need him and never had. Sure, she was under threat from serial killer Boyd Sullivan along with a list of others who'd crossed him, but the investigative team Ethan was a part of would catch him. Besides, Jillian was a woman who could take care of herself—ruthless, determined and entirely self-absorbed. She'd been offered protection after Sullivan killed two K-9 handlers at Canyon Air Force Base, including Ethan's best friend, Airman Landon Martelli. He'd also murdered Chief Master Sergeant Clint Lockwood in the same killing spree. She'd declined the protection in spite of the risks. No surprise there.

Sullivan's not smart enough to hurt me, she'd said. Typical.

Yet all of a sudden Jillian had just gone along with her father hiring a look-alike as bait? Insane. He slammed a hand on the steering wheel. Titus regarded him from the passenger seat, head cocked, ears flopping as if to say, "What's going on?"

In the six years they'd trained, lived and served together, including their last deployment to Afghanistan, Titus could read Ethan better than any other living creature. And now that they shared a living space, the bond had grown stronger. Sullivan's break-in at Canyon Air Force Base had had other disastrous results besides the deaths of human personnel. Sullivan had let loose nearly two hundred dogs from the Military Working Dogs training center. Twenty-eight of them had yet to be found.

Ethan had been given special permission to keep Titus with him instead of at the kennel until the repairs could be done and security assured.

That was fine by Ethan, as he was cross-training Titus as a cadaver detection dog in addition to his patrol duties. The more time they spent together the better. Plus, military dogs were more than just animals, they were partners. And he had to be sure his partner was protected. Titus had his back and Ethan returned the favor.

"I've gotta talk this nutty lady out of standing in for Jillian before she gets herself killed," he muttered.

Titus flapped his ears and settled back into the seat.

Preparing his most convincing argument for Kendra, he waited for her to exit the office. He was surprised when she stepped out lugging some sort of small animal carrier. He started to exit the vehicle to talk to her, but she loaded the carrier and slid behind the wheel of her car so quickly he didn't have the chance. As she drove by, he caught her profile, her long red hair now captured in a tight twist at the nape of a graceful neck, a spray of freckles across the nose. His stomach dropped. So like Jillian. Anger choked him, and hurt speared through him as sharp as it had been the day he'd finally understood how his wife had betrayed him, repeatedly, and he'd been nothing but gullible and blind to it. What a sap. Dense as his aunt Millie's fruitcake.

"Let it go," he commanded himself. "You've been divorced for three years. She's not your problem anymore." He decided that with his current state of mind it was best not to head back to Canyon until he got his anger under control and then sorted out how to get Kendra Bell out of the picture.

He pulled out of the parking lot and took the back road off the Marine base, bathed in shadows from the trees that broke up the buttery June sunlight. Unseasonably hot, people were saying, which made him laugh. After returning from Afghanistan, where the temps could top 115 degrees before noon, he'd never complain about the Texas heat again.

Titus seemed to feel the same, stretched out to catch the sunshine, enjoying the moments free from enemy sniper fire and the constant tension born of living in a war zone. Titus was a top-notch patrol dog, sniffing out hidden insurgents and intruders at checkpoints, and he was taking easily to his new training in cadaver detection. The animal's incredible abilities never ceased to boggle Ethan's mind. God knew what He was doing when he made dogs.

The miles rolled by along with his thoughts until he was surprised to catch up to Kendra as she headed into a curvy, wooded section of road. A slow and careful driver, unlike the woman she resembled. The bumper of her car disappeared around a turn and gunfire ripped through the air, followed by the sound of breaking glass. Adrenaline exploded through his body as he floored the accelerator, stopping just in time to see Kendra's vehicle skid off the road and down the slope. He pulled the truck behind a pile of rocks and dialed both 911 and Masters's direct line. Titus went rigid, ears erect, nose twitching, waiting for a signal from Ethan. Messages delivered, there was no more time to spare. Kendra might be badly injured.

Clipping on Titus's lead, he unlocked the box from under his seat and slipped the handgun in his belt. Slamming the door, he sprinted toward the edge where her car had gone over, praying the sniper's bullets had not found their target.

Was Sullivan making his move already? Kendra fought the bucking steering wheel after the last shot had taken out the front tire. Then again, she had another enemy hot on her trail. She didn't know that Andy was a good enough shot to take out a tire, but he was skilled at many other means of inflicting pain. Whether it was Sullivan or Andy didn't really matter at the moment. She battled for control of her vehicle, but there was no time. The car bumped and jolted, skidding sideways toward the trees. "Hold on, Baby," she shouted to the elderly cat tucked in his back seat carrier. Her words were lost in the jolt of the chassis as it smacked against the rocky ground. Thick tree trunks flashed past the windows as the car flew down the slope, gravity overwhelming the brakes. The front fender slammed into a pile of rocks so hard it snapped her neck back and drove the breath out of her. For several seconds all she could do was cling to the steering wheel, wondering why the airbag hadn't deployed.

"Baby?" she finally croaked. "Are you okay?"

With a painful effort, she unbuckled her seat belt, grabbed her Glock and turned to peer over the headrest into the back seat. Her heart pounded at what she might find in the cat carrier.

Please, God, don't let Baby be dead. I know I don't deserve to ask You for anything, not one thing, but I'm asking anyway. The silence from the rear of the car galvanized her into action.

Shoving an elbow at the door, she forced it open, tumbling to her knees on the rocky ground. Pain in her ribs made her gasp but she pulled herself up and grabbed the rear door handle.

The crunch of footsteps made her draw back.

Sullivan or Andy?

Andy's last voice mail message echoed in her ears. *When I finally catch up to you, I am going to enjoy killing you slowly.*

She gritted her teeth. If he was going to kill her today, she'd make sure it would be the hardest thing he'd ever done.

The sounds drew nearer. Her mind sought options. Flag someone down? Ethan had been behind her for a while, she'd noticed, but she'd lost sight of him a few miles back. Incredibly, she heard no traffic at all on this back road out of the Baylor Marine Corps Base. She reached for her cell phone when she heard a whispered voice.

"Kendra?"

The voice didn't belong to Andy, that was certain. This voice was a low baritone, complete with a Tennessee drawl. Ethan. She let out a slow breath.

"I'm coming over to you," he continued, "so don't do anything crazy like shoot me."

She kept silent, gripping the Glock and training the

gun toward the direction of the shots. Ethan rounded the corner with a dog at his side. The pointer immediately stiffened, ears erect.

"I don't like dogs," she snapped.

"That's okay. He probably doesn't like you, either. Cops and marines should be on their way."

"What are you doing here?" She shot a look at the animal still in alert position. A patrol or scout dog, she suspected.

He quirked an eyebrow. "Maybe we can do the pleasantries later? After the cavalry arrives?"

She would have retorted, but a shot whistled through the air and they hunkered low for cover.

"Sullivan doesn't usually do his dirty work in public," he said over his shoulder, peering in the direction of the shooter. "Anyone else you know who might shooting at you?"

"Could be anyone," she said, earning another exasperated look.

"You can play innocent with me, but I don't think the marines are gonna be as warm and fuzzy."

"If you think you're warm and fuzzy," she said, yanking the back door handle, "then you're pretty clueless."

He put out a hand to stop her. "Leave it. We have to move. Shooter is going to change locations to get a better bead now that we're pinned down."

She ignored him, pulling harder on the door, which opened with a reluctant groan.

He grabbed her forearm. "Didn't you hear me?"

"Hearing and listening are two different things."

A shot drilled the rear window, sending glass rocketing in all directions. They both ducked.

"You're really stubborn," he said, but she was already

lugging the animal carrier out of the car, and he reached in to help.

Another shot pinged the metal car roof, sending off sparks.

"Come on," he said, taking her arm and propelling her toward the shrubbery.

It was all she could do to hold on to the carrier.

"I thought MPs were supposed to stand their ground," she huffed.

"We do, but this isn't my ground and I happen to be saddled with an irrational civilian."

So much for warm and fuzzy.

He pushed her ahead of him, and he and the dog took up position right behind her as another volley of shots bored into the tree just above their heads.

TWO

Ethan put as many sturdy tree trunks between them and the shooter as he could. His mind churned faster than his feet. Had Sullivan finally snapped and changed his tactics to include daylight ambushes? It was possible. Sullivan wasn't much of a shot, he happened to know, and this gunman was all over the place. Two more bullets whistled by, the last a wild one that lost itself in the tree branches. Sirens were converging from all directions. The marines would be responding, and the local police. With that many guns and that much adrenaline pumping, he figured their safest option was to stay still, very still. He put Titus into a sit.

"Stay put," he told the woman. "Marines are here."

The Jillian look-alike stood with her back to a tree, her arms curled around the animal carrier. Now that he got a close look without a couple of feet between them, he could see that her mouth was fuller than Jillian's, the hair more auburn than copper, the spray of freckles more subtle, but still...uncanny.

"Still staring?" she demanded.

He flushed. "How do you know Jillian?"

A flash of emotion crossed her face, indicating that whatever her connection was to Jillian, it was a strong one. Then the expression disappeared and she shrugged. "Friends."

His instincts went berserk, as if he was inches from stepping into a trip wire, but he had to know. "You're a pretty good friend to paint a target on your back."

She flashed a smile this time as she pointed to several armed marines scurrying down the slope, geared up for battle. "I think that conversation is going to have to wait."

She was right. The marines were in no mood for chatting. Once they ascertained that Kendra and Ethan were not the bad guys, they searched the area until the police arrived, finding no sign of the shooter.

One marine approached them. "Hey, Airman. Heard you slammed the door on Colonel Masters an hour ago."

Ethan grinned at the marine police captain, friends from the time their deployments overlapped. "News travels fast, Hector."

MP Marine Captain Hector Sanchez squashed his smile and regarded the woman next to him intently. "Your name, ma'am?"

"Kendra. I had a meeting on base with Lieutenant Colonel Terence Masters."

He raised an eyebrow. "Pertaining to?"

"Ask him, if you want to know."

"Due respect, ma'am, but we're not in the mood for coy around here."

Ethan wasn't, either. He was in the mood for a little rest and recuperation before he threw himself back into the Red Rose Killer investigation. Now that he was working for Masters, the situation was changing from bad to atrocious. The good news was Kendra would have to come to her senses now and tell Masters she was quitting.

Hector greeted the arriving police officer and they launched into an intense conversation. The US Marines did not like having to relinquish any authority to the local cops, but the shooting was not technically on base property. The cop, whose name tag read Alonso Carpenter, drew Ethan and Kendra aside. He was a tall man, almost as tall as Ethan, with a narrow chin and skin tanned from the sun.

"We need to have a talk back at the station with you both, to document all the details," he said.

"It this really necessary?" Kendra's arms were still wrapped around the carrier as if she was holding on to a life preserver. "I'm sure Colonel Masters—"

"Masters," Carpenter said, with a certain something in his voice, "is not the boss on this side of the fence."

Ethan caught the grin on Hector's face. He realized he was sporting the same smug smile on his own. Masters always got what he wanted one way or another by whatever means necessary. It was nice to know the local police did not jump when he snapped his fingers.

He wanted nothing more than to head back to his apartment at Canyon Air Force Base and forget the whole nutty plan, but perhaps Masters's scheme would actually draw Boyd out. It was possible the shooting had been Sullivan's work. But something still didn't feel right. Sullivan was not the type to take shots from the bushes. His killings were up close and personal. Ethan's stomach tensed thinking of how Sullivan had snuffed out the life of his friend Landon Martelli. Landon hadn't even had a chance to defend himself.

If it wasn't Sullivan, then who else might want Kendra dead and why? He shook away the thought. *Not your problem, Webb.* He wasn't going to work with Kendra Bell only to see her become another victim of Sullivan's, and he intended to force her to see reality one way or another. The best thing for her would be to get away from this part of Texas, and especially from Masters.

Kendra walked by him and slid into a waiting police car. She did not flash him a glance, just bent her head and cooed to the bony white cat she'd removed from the carrier.

He could see that her profile wasn't exactly a match for Jillian's; her nose was smaller, the cheeks softer and there was more delicacy about this woman than his ex-wife. Her hair looked soft, as if it would be silky under his fingertips.

He brought those thoughts sharply to heel, calling to Titus, who had been nosing along at the tufts of grass. A moment later the cat caught sight of Titus and mewed in fright.

Startled, Titus barked loud enough to make Ethan's ears ring. The cat erupted from Kendra's arms and streaked away into the woods.

"Baby," Kendra screamed, leaping from the car. She fired an angry look at Ethan. "Can't you control your brute of a dog?" she said before she ran away in search of the cat.

"What?" he said dumbly to her back.

"She said, 'Can't you control your brute of a dog?'" Officer Carpenter said and Ethan detected a look of enjoyment in the man's eyes.

Ethan huffed out a breath and shot a glare at Titus. The dog blinked and looked away as if to say, "Sorry, but it was a cat, after all." Then he noticed the officer was heading into the shrubbery.

"Aren't you taking her to the station?" Ethan called.

Carpenter chuckled. "Son, I've been married twice and I'd like to think I've learned a thing or two. I think I can safely say that Ms. Bell isn't going anywhere with-out that cat."

"Does that mean I can go and you'll call me when you're ready to talk to me?"

Carpenter raised an eyebrow. "No, that means you and Wonder Dog are going to comb every inch of this property until you locate the cat, Airman." He turned his back and left Ethan and Titus standing there.

Ethan turned to his dog. "This is your fault, you know."

Titus licked Ethan's hand.

"Don't try to act all cute now. Get into those bushes and find the cat you just bullied."

Titus put his nose to the ground and got to work.

Kendra's cheek was scratched from a low-lying branch and her feet were aching since she was wearing ballet flats instead of hiking boots. It didn't hold a candle to the pain inside her. Baby was gone. The sun was low in the sky and there was still no sign of the old cat.

The cop had trudged back to the car after she'd prom-ised to follow in five more minutes. With each second her breathing grew more panicky, sweat making her palms clammy. Ethan and Titus continued to prowl through the bushes, but even the dog could not seem to catch a scent of Baby.

Ethan clumped out of the bushes, wiping sweat from his brow, and faced her. "Uh, I'm sorry your cat ran away," he said, not exactly looking her in the eye.

She rounded on him. "She didn't run away. Your dog scared her."

Now he turned eyes the color of melted chocolate in her direction. "Look, I'm really sorry, okay? I'll keep searching, or maybe I can get you another cat."

"Another cat?" she snapped, fury taking her breath away. "And if Titus there got lost, you'd just give up on him and get another dog?"

"No way, but Titus is a dog. I mean, uh, what I meant was, you know, cats can take care of themselves."

She stared at him, tears pricking her eyes. "For your information, Baby can't. She's sixteen and she's in poor health. She's been the only one…" She swallowed hard. There was no way she was going to unload all of her big fat messed-up life at the feet of this insensitive blockhead. "Never mind." She stalked past him, but he grasped her arm, his fingers strong but gentle.

"Hey, wait. I'm sorry. I was being a jerk. I've only been back a couple of months and I think I'm rusty at some things. I know the cat means a lot to you." His gaze was soft, or maybe it was a trick of the failing sunlight. Either way, she couldn't answer over the thick lump in her throat.

"I…" He sighed and shook his head, letting her go. "I lost a dog before Titus to a grenade. It hurts, no matter how you lose them. I, um, I'll keep looking. Give me your cell phone number and I'll text you if…I mean, when I find her, okay?"

Still unsure of her powers of speech, Kendra managed to give Ethan her cell number and programmed his into her phone.

"Ms. Bell?" Officer Carpenter called. "It's time to go."

She raised her chin and blinked hard, fighting for composure as she allowed the cop to usher her into his car.

Sitting next to the empty carrier, she was overwhelmed by the thoughts that she'd been blotting out the last few hours. Someone—maybe Andy, maybe the Red Rose Killer, maybe none of the above—had tried to kill her. That was not a new experience for a private investigator and a former bounty hunter, but this person had gotten very close to getting the job done. Muscles deep in her belly began to quiver.

And now Baby, the only creature in the world whom she loved and who loved her back, was gone, lost in the woods, an old cat, easy prey. She squeezed her hands together to stop the shaking.

You'll find her, she told herself savagely. *Right after the police interview you'll come back and you'll find her.* Baby had chosen somewhere to hide, that was all.

Lord, she prayed, *bring Baby back and help us both find a place like that.*

As they drove through the shadows, her newfound faith was not enough to screen out the memory of the bullets fracturing the windshield, boring into the trees.

She was just like the cat. Easy prey.

THREE

After hours of fruitless searching Ethan made it back to Canyon Air Force Base. He'd done his best, but there was simply no sign of the cat. Titus was ready for a cold drink of water and some grub and so was he. Maybe in the morning...

As he unloaded Titus from the truck, they both caught the sound of whimpering coming from the bushes in his front yard. Titus dashed toward the foliage, tail wagging. Ethan followed, getting down on his knees as the soft cries turned into full-blown yips.

Titus was nose to nose with a gangly puppy, a Malinois with pointy ears and a dark muzzle. The ears were erect and the tongue was out, busily bathing Titus.

"Hey, fella," Ethan said. "How did you get here?" He was close enough now to see that the puppy was wearing a filthy training center collar.

Ethan's throat constricted. It was one of the animals that had been let loose by Boyd Sullivan when he killed the two K-9 trainers and left his signature red rose calling card. With Titus's encouragement, he coaxed the dog to come out. It didn't take much, as the poor critter was clearly weak and terrified. The pup was skinny, his ribs protruding. He smelled of garbage, which was where he'd probably been scrounging for food to stay alive for so long. Ethan noted a long gash in the dog's side. His anger at Sullivan kindled fresh and hot. How could a guy who'd once wanted to become a K-9 trainer let hundreds of dogs loose to be injured or worse? But Sullivan's twisted sense of revenge didn't stop there. He'd killed a commissary cook a few miles from base, and some of those in his basic training flight group had received roses and threats…including Jillian.

Ethan poured some water from a bottle into his cupped palm and the dog lapped at it eagerly while Titus gave him a thorough sniffing. Wrapping the pup in his jacket, Ethan ignored the growling in his stomach and loaded both dogs into the truck.

In twenty minutes he was pulling up to the K-9 training center. He'd called Master Sergeant Westley James and his new wife, base photographer Staff Sergeant Felicity James, on the way. At the entrance to the training yard, Westley waited, a head taller than the petite Felicity, his face grave.

"Another one found," Felicity said, cooing to the puppy. "He's skin and bones. I'll get him to the clinic."

Westley shook his head. "If I could just get a lead on Sullivan…"

"You and everyone else," Ethan said. "We're all hoping to be the one that brings him down."

"And his accomplice," Felicity added. "He isn't doing all these things without help."

Someone was helping Sullivan certainly, but the list of suspects shifted constantly, and the team assembled to track down the killer was growing more and more frustrated.

Trainer Rusty Morton rushed over, tossing the rag he'd been using on the ground. "Oh, man. Is that Rocket?

I heard he'd been sighted on and off in the woods and raiding garbage cans. I left out food and water where they said they'd spotted him." He leaned over to stroke the dog's ears tenderly. "I didn't think I'd ever see you again, buddy."

Puzzlement played across Felicity's face as she handed the dog into Rusty's arms. "Hang on to him for a minute while I alert the vet, okay?"

Ethan shared her uncertainty. Rusty was on the list of Sullivan's potential accomplices, under scrutiny from the investigation team as he'd been a friend of Boyd Sullivan's during their basic training days.

But Ethan saw tears shining in the guy's eyes. They weren't fake, he was certain. That contradicted Ethan's earlier suspicions. He made a note to mention it to the investigative team leader Captain Blackwood. Surely a guy who loved dogs as much as Rusty wouldn't have helped Sullivan let the animals loose, would he?

Ethan thought about his friend Landon. Man, he missed talking to him about anything and everything.

"You okay?" Felicity asked.

"Yeah." He shrugged. "Just thinking about Martelli."

"We miss him, too," she said quietly.

Ethan's phone rang and he moved away to answer it, Titus roaming the enclosed yard.

"Heard you got into some trouble near Baylor, Lieutenant," Justin Blackwood said. He was a captain in the Security Forces and a veteran of two tours of duty in Afghanistan, which gave him stellar credentials in Ethan's book, the perfect guy to be the leader of the team trying to hunt down Boyd Sullivan. "Was the shooting Sullivan's work?"

"Uncertain, sir. Doesn't seem like his MO." Ethan felt the tension crackling through the phone.

"I wouldn't rule it out completely. Sullivan was spotted near Baylor Marine Corps Base hours prior to your shooting incident."

Ethan's pulse ticked up a notch as Blackwood continued.

"A marine has been killed off base, his uniform and ID are gone."

Ethan's stomach dropped at the news of another murder. And now Sullivan had access to the base and Kendra. Perhaps the shooting really was a case of mistaken identity?

"We've got our hands full on this case," Blackwood said. "I know you'd rather be doing anything other than working with Jillian and Masters, but maybe you can find that lead we're all looking for."

"I'll do what I can, sir," he said.

"Fair enough. Keep me posted."

"Yes, sir," Ethan said, disconnecting.

His eyes landed on Rusty as he cooed to the pup, who looked half-starved in the training center lights. Immediately he thought about Kendra cradling the pet carrier, tears glistening in her eyes, knowing her cat was lost like Rocket had been.

Your fault, Ethan.

On impulse, he sent her a text.

Did you find your cat?

Should he add something like another apology? An "I hope so" or something to soften it?

"I'm glad to have Rocket returned," Westley said. "But there are still plenty of dogs on the loose as well as a serial killer." He looped a protective arm around Felicity's shoulders.

A text materialized on Ethan's cell phone screen.

No.

He imagined Kendra's lip caught between her teeth, a sheen of moisture in those brown eyes, the same brown as the glossy acorns that festooned the trees on his mother's property back home.

She's been the only one... Kendra had said of Baby, and he thought he had an inkling about the rest. The only one to understand, to listen to the painful things that could not be spoken to human listeners, the only one who did not judge, did not condemn. He got it. Titus had heard more about Ethan's life story than anyone, except for the One who'd seen him through it.

He nodded to Felicity and Westley. "Okay. Thanks for taking care of Rocket. I've got to get on the road."

"Where to?" Felicity asked him.

"Back to Baylor."

She quirked a look at him. "That's a three-hour drive. Didn't you just get back from there?"

"Yeah," he said, with a weary sigh. *But I've got to go find a cat.*

Kendra had finally returned to Jillian's rented home just outside base property somewhere after 7:00 p.m. It would be a short break to wolf down a granola bar and rehydrate. Then five minutes to change clothes and grab her pack and then she would search again for Baby. It was only another hour until sunset. Her stomach churned into nausea.

"Hang on, sweetie. I'm coming to get you."

A knock at the door startled her. She pulled the curtain aside a crack. Ethan Webb stood on the doorstep, arms crossed, expression stony.

What now? She had no time for another row with him. She yanked the door open, staring him down. "Come to apologize?"

He quirked a brow. "For what?"

"Disrespecting me in front of my boss. Scaring my cat."

"Disrespecting…" He rubbed a hand over his tanned face. "Whatever. We just have one piece of business left and then I'm hoping you'll see reason and quit this job."

She shook her head.

"You can't trust Masters," he said. "Get away from him as quick as you can. This situation is only going to get you hurt or killed."

"Thanks for your concern, but you didn't have to drive over here to tell me that. I've known Jillian for fifteen years so I'm well aware that her father is a manipulative man with no ethics."

He gaped. "Then why would you work for him?"

Because I owe his daughter my life. She shrugged. "Not your business, but thanks for dropping by."

"So you're still going to persist in acting as a decoy for Sullivan?"

"Yes."

His lips thinned, his nostrils flared and he started to speak, stopped, then started again, folding his arms across his broad chest.

Amused, she folded her arms to mirror his. "Cat got your tongue?"

"Wait here," he snapped.

She was about to respond when he stalked to his car. Titus sat in the passenger seat, ears alert, snout poking through the open window. He reached into the back and returned with a blanket, pushing the bundle into her arms.

Her heart stopped at the sight of Baby, mewing plaintively. She could not hold back the tears that filled her eyes as she snuggled the cat under her chin. "You found her."

He shrugged. "Cost me a couple hours of searching and a million mosquito bites, but yeah. Baby's back. Titus was not thrilled about sharing his vehicle with a cat, but he's grounded so he doesn't get to complain about it."

She laughed. "Thank you, Lieutenant."

"You can call me Ethan," he said. "I guess we'll be stuck in this idiotic mission together if you won't listen to reason." With a sigh, he started to walk away.

"Wait." She put a hand on his shoulder, muscles hard under her touch, and he turned back halfway. "I'm sorry for my rudeness. I really do appreciate what you did, more than I can put into words. Baby is...so much more than just a cat to me."

She thought his cheeks might have pinked a bit, but she could not tell for certain. He blew out a breath and he turned to face her fully.

"I'm serious here. I know we got snarled up in the beginning, but Masters is trouble and so is his daughter. Neither of them cares who gets hurt, so long as they get what they want. You are expendable and so am I, do you get that?"

If she wasn't mistaken, she thought she saw a deep-down pain shimmer in his eyes before he cleared his throat. She nodded. "I understand."

His gaze lingered, poring over her face from under a thick fringe of lashes. "Okay, well, it's late," he said. "We can work out the nuts and bolts tomorrow. Call if you need...you know...anything."

He hesitated.

"Something else you wanted to say?" she said.

He held up his palms. "Now don't get a burr under your saddle about it, but did you check the house? Make sure the doors and windows are secure?"

She grimaced, wishing she could have answered yes. "Um, actually, I was in such a hurry to go searching for Baby, I didn't. I'm sure Jillian checked before she left." *Some PI you are, Kendra.*

"Want me to…?"

"No," she said firmly. "I can handle it, thank you."

"All right, then." He walked the few steps to his truck, where he leaned against the front fender. "Just wave at me when you get it done and I'll scoot."

"You always this pushy?"

"I'm as calm as clam shells on most days, but when there's a serial killer roaming around, I get a little testy."

Though his posture was relaxed, long legs stretched out, boots crossed at the ankles, she had a feeling he would stay there until she reported that the house was secure. Period.

"I'll just be a minute." Blowing out a breath she made a quick check of the tiny front room and the kitchen, depositing Baby on the linoleum with a bowl of water and some kitty kibble. It warmed her insides to see Baby chowing down with gusto. She felt a deep surge of gratitude toward Ethan that, for the moment, outweighed her frustration with him.

Kendra moved onto a small bedroom being used as a study. The area was sparse, minimally decorated, as was in keeping with Jillian's unsentimental personality. Jillian hadn't said exactly where she was staying while Kendra lived at her place, only that she'd keep in touch by phone. Jillian was not touchy-feely about friendships, either. When Kendra paid back the debt she owed Jillian for saving her life that long-ago summer day when she'd helped her escape from Andy, she suspected there would be no further connection between them.

Kendra hastened to the back of the house to check the master bedroom. She reached out a hand to push open the door and something large and soft fell from above. A paper sack split as it hit the floor and suddenly the room was alive with enraged wasps streaming out of a fragment of wasp nest.

In her panic, Kendra stumbled and fell backward, screaming as the stinging insects swarmed over her.

FOUR

Ethan slammed through the front door at the first scream. He was down the hall and unexpectedly battling his way through angry wasps that thickened as he reached the bedroom. Kendra was on her hands and knees, crawling toward the threshold, insects enveloping her, trying to get her feet underneath her to escape. He caught hold of her arm and hauled her out of the room, slamming the door, which confined most of the vicious creatures. The remaining few continued to sting both of them, jabbing repeatedly. He killed as many as he could while they stumbled to the kitchen. Closing the swinging door, he grabbed the nearest weapon, a pot holder. With a startled mew, Baby scuttled under the nearest chair while he swatted the wasps that hovered over Kendra, trying not to hurt her.

Tears of pain streamed down her cheeks and red welts began to appear here and there along her arms.

"I think I got them," he said. He scanned feverishly until he realized there were more wasps tangled in her red hair.

"Quit wiggling," he commanded.

She twitched and flailed. "You try it sometime."

Commandeering her into a chair, he shooed the insects from the silky mass and squashed them.

Ethan and Kendra sat still, listening for more.

She breathed hard. "Somebody—" she swallowed "—somebody put the nest there, above the door."

Somebody? He filled a plastic bag with ice from the tiny freezer and gave it to her. "Hold this to the stings on your face. It was only some of the colony in that bag, fortunately. Looks like only half a dozen stings."

He filled another and grasped her forearm as gently as he could. He applied the cold to the worst of the welts. "Are you allergic to insect bites?"

"Guess we're about to find out," she said, a wry twist on her lips.

He grinned back. The lady had gumption. He'd known grown men so scared of wasps they ran at the first sight of one. "So who's the 'someone'?"

She looked at the floor. "What do you mean?"

"You know what I mean, so don't play clueless. This isn't the Red Rose Killer. This is personal, very personal, intended to shake you up, but probably not to kill you outright. So who's the someone who wants to torture you?"

Her swollen eyes weighed and measured him, like he had weighed and measured so many of the people he'd interrogated as a military cop. To trust, or not? It wouldn't surprise him if she decided not to, in light of their contentious relations to date. Her gaze shifted to Baby, who was lying flat on the linoleum, tracking a stray wasp that traversed the kitchen. He could read the emotions flickering across her face. He'd saved her cat, a creature who obviously meant everything to her. Decision made.

Kendra let out a breath that came out as a sigh. "My former boyfriend," she said. "Andy Bleakman."

He waited, silent, sensing there was more coming.

"He did prison time because of me."

"Why?"

Her cheeks blushed crimson to match her red welts. "I don't want to go into it now."

"No better time."

She yanked her arm from his grasp. "I've just been a wasp pin cushion and the bedroom is still full of angry insects, so I contend there is a better time. As a matter of fact, any time would be better than this time."

He liked the fire in her voice, the way she lifted that delicate chin and stared him down. It made his pulse kick up one notch.

Back off, Ethan. No more hotheaded women for you, especially one who is the spitting image of Jillian. He cleared his throat. "Just give me the critical points then. What was Andy in prison for?"

A beat of hesitation told him her trust only went so far. "Armed robbery."

"And he blames you."

"Yes. Jillian helped me get away from him, so now revenge on me is his mission in life."

Jillian helped? He considered that. Throughout their marriage Jillian had been busily helping herself, chasing after every adrenaline-fueled thrill she could get her hands on, but she also had a desperate need to be the hero. He could imagine her riding to the rescue of her helpless friend…and then discarding her like a used dishrag when she'd finished. Mouth open, he was just about to tell Kendra so, when it dawned on him that she looked plumb worn-out.

He went to the truck and let Titus into the backyard, filling a bowl of water for him and another with kibble. Returning to the kitchen, he palmed his phone.

"Who are you calling?"

"Pest control to come and retrieve your wasp nest." Ear to the phone, he strode to the refrigerator and opened it.

"Looking for something?" she said, brows quirked.

He poked around inside. "It'll do."

"Do for what?"

"Dinner. I'm hungry."

She gaped. "Are you expecting me to cook you dinner?"

"No, ma'am," he said. "I'm gonna do the cooking while you go wash your face and make sure you got all the wasps out of your clothes." He pointed to a door. "Laundry room?"

"Yes."

"There are no wasps in there and you probably have extra clothes there already."

She pursed her lips. "So…you can cook, Lieutenant?"

"Call me Ethan, and I happen to be an excellent cook thanks to my mama, who won so many blue ribbons at the fair I lost count." He gestured to the laundry room. "Get a move on."

"Are military cops always so bossy?"

"Only the good ones. Go. Pest control is on the way." He pulled the eggs from the fridge and began to prowl for a frying pan. Before she left, he'd located a spatula and brandished it like bayonet. "I'm armed and dangerous."

She smiled, as he'd hoped she would. "Okay. Be right back."

"Kendra?"

"Yes?"

"You said you're Andy's mission in life. What exactly does that mean?"

She rubbed at a welt on her cheek, eyes gone dark.

"He's going to make sure that I suffer before he kills me." Shoulders bowed, she left.

So the man with a mission to hurt Kendra knew where she lived, and how to get into her house. Was he also the one who'd taken shots at her vehicle? Or could it be that Boyd Sullivan was changing things up, trying out new ways to torture his victims before he killed them?

The case was turning into a many-headed monster.

Monsters didn't scare Ethan one bit. There was no enemy that he and Titus couldn't put down.

Whistling, he set to work on the eggs.

She wouldn't admit it, but Kendra was thrilled to strip off her clothes and change into clean jeans and a T-shirt. The welts on her arms were red and angry, but they did not seem to be affecting her breathing. Her face was probably a mess, so she was grateful there wasn't a mirror in the laundry room. Part of her tensed at the thought of Ethan Webb clanging pots and pans in her kitchen. The last thing she wanted was a partner—a handsome, pushy, military partner with whom she'd already shared way more than she wanted to. The other part of her recalled the image of him dragging her away from the wasps with no concern for himself.

The minute she returned to the kitchen, Ethan gestured her into a chair and slid a plate with a perfectly golden wedge in front of her.

"Wow. That looks great."

"It is. Frittata without mushrooms 'cuz you didn't have any." His brash tone made her smile. "You should keep mushrooms on hand. Very versatile."

"I'll make a note of it. I only just arrived here last night, so I didn't have time for much shopping."

He sat across from her and to her surprise, he took her hand to give thanks.

"Lord, thanks for giving us this good food and another day to enjoy it."

After the "amen" he grinned. "Sorry. I shoulda asked if you wanted to say it."

"Is that your subtle way of asking if I'm a believer?"

"Are you?"

"Yes. A new one, I'm afraid."

He laughed. "Doesn't matter if you're new or got some miles behind you. Truth is truth, no matter when you arrive at it."

"Texas wisdom?"

He grimaced in mock affront. "Tennessee, ma'am. We got lots of wisdom there, way more than here in Texas."

She dug into the fritatta, redolent with red peppers and onions. "You really are a good cook."

"Yes, ma'am, I am," he said.

"And humble, too."

"Upon occasion."

Kendra laughed. A soft knock sounded on the kitchen door and she was surprised to find a small woman, late thirties maybe, standing on the porch, her long brown hair caught in a ponytail. She held out a plastic bag of cherries. Her blue eyes were wide with alarm as she got a look at Kendra.

"Are you… I mean, are you okay, Jillian? Your face… is a little swollen."

Kendra snapped herself back into the role she should have been playing all along, thankful for her swollen face. "Oh, yes, I'm okay." She put a finger to her cheek. "I got tangled up with some wasps." She turned to Ethan. "Ethan, this is Mindy Zeppler, my next-door neighbor."

"We've only had a chance to say hi in passing," Mindy said. "You're so busy, Jillian."

Another blessing, Kendra realized. Jillian and Mindy hadn't spent time together, which made her more likely to accept Kendra as Jillian.

"I, uh, I heard you and Ethan were divorced. It's nice to see you still get along so well."

In one swift movement, Ethan stepped close to Kendra and looped an arm around her. "Reconciled, ma'am. We're both thrilled to be together again." He pressed a kiss to the temple free of stings and her blood raced right up to her face. "Can't believe we wasted so much time," he said as he leaned in closer, his breath warm on her neck.

Kendra's body prickled all over and chills raced up her spine. What was he doing?

Mindy smiled at Ethan. "Your dog is beautiful. Patrol dog?"

"And soon to be cadaver detector," he said proudly.

Mindy's mouth dropped open.

Titus's new skill was a real conversation stopper, Kendra realized.

"I was just bringing by some cherries. Nice to meet you, Ethan. I work for a real estate business in town. I can ask them about a good pest control guy." She shivered. "Wasps are the worst. They just keep stinging until they're dead."

Or their victim is, Kendra thought with a shudder. "We'll take care of it." She was not certain how much to tell Mindy, but in her experience as a private investigator, the less information she let spill the better. "Thanks, though, for bringing the cherries."

"Would you care for some frittata, ma'am?" Ethan was acting the perfect Southern gentleman.

Mindy waved a hand. "Oh, no, thank you, I just came to deliver a message with the cherries."

"A message?" Kendra felt an inexplicable chill.

"Yes, a man called me yesterday." She frowned. "I'm not sure how he got my number, now that I think about it. He said he was an old friend of yours and he was trying to find you."

"Did he leave his name?"

"No. I figured you were US Marine buddies."

"What made you think that, ma'am?" Ethan's voice as level and low, but intense.

"Well…" Mindy said, her mouth crimped as she thought about it. "I'm not sure. He was polite, like you, though no accent. Maybe I just imagined the marine thing because I know you're a pilot," she said to Kendra.

"Ma'am, would you happen to have that number on your phone?" Ethan asked her.

She shook her head. "It said, 'Unknown Caller.' I deleted it. I'm sorry. Is it important?"

Ethan shrugged. "It's okay."

"What was the message?" Kendra asked.

"He said to tell you he was looking forward to seeing you again soon and he was going to bring you some roses. I thought it was sweet."

Roses.
Sullivan.
Looking forward to seeing you again.
Soon.

FIVE

Kendra waited until Mindy was safely gone and pest control had cleaned up the nest before she drummed up the courage to face Ethan.

"Ethan, this isn't going to work."

"What isn't?" he said as he fastened a harness on Titus.

"This...pretend marriage thing."

He stopped and looked at her. "Oh. Did I freak you out?"

Was there a challenge in his voice? "No, you didn't. It's just that, I mean, it might be hard to convince people."

"Not for me. I'm—"

She rolled her eyes. "Let me guess, a great actor? In addition to being a good cook and a top-notch MP?"

His smile was warm and honey-sweet. "I was gonna say I'm not too proud to play the part of a love-struck fella if it will bag us Sullivan. Besides, you smell nice."

She blinked. "What?"

"You smell nice, like cinnamon or something. I noticed when I kissed you." He finished clasping on Titus's harness.

"You...you shouldn't be kissing me at all," she snapped out. *And I shouldn't be liking it!*

That got his attention. "You don't think we'd be kissing if we're gonna get remarried?"

"We're not going to get remarried, or date, or anything like that." Her face was now scarlet, she had no doubt.

He got to his feet. "All right, ma'am." He led Titus to the door, moving closer to her in order to edge around the chairs. "Have it your way, but for the record, you do smell nice."

Leaving her gaping, he led Titus outside. Thoughts zinging, she followed. *Be professional, Kendra. If he can focus on the job, so can you.* Obviously the kiss hadn't meant a thing to Ethan other than giving him a chance to sniff her, just like Titus. Maybe there was truth to the saying that men were dogs.

Ethan did a walk around the outside of the house. It gave her a small measure of comfort to be doing something, even as trivial as securing the yard. The knowledge that Sullivan was closing in sent her skin prickling. Or was it Andy? She didn't understand why Sullivan would have gone to the trouble to plant a wasp nest in her house, but it made perfect sense for Andy to have done so. She had calls in to check if he had reported for his mandated appointment with his parole officer in northern Texas. If he hadn't, then he might very well have come hunting for her. The air took on a sudden chill.

The ground around the outside of Jillian's small house gave up nothing of interest, no footprints, not so much as a blade of grass out of place. The only sign of an intruder was the bedroom window. Scratch marks and chipped paint indicated where the intruder had used a pry bar to force the old lock and gain entry. It must have been awkward, breaking and entering and transporting a wasp nest.

Titus paced around in Ethan's wake.

"Why is your dog whining?"

"He's a little off his game. Used to being kenneled at

night, so now that he isn't, he has to be in close proximity to me when the sun goes down or he gets nervous."

"So you're a six-foot security blankie for your dog?"

"Six foot four."

She laughed. "You're a big baby, Titus."

The dog gave her a pitiful glance.

"That look usually results in people giving him ear rubs, if I allow it."

Kendra just shook her head. "Told you I'm not susceptible to canine manipulation."

"Just feline wiles?"

"Baby is too old to be sneaky. How exactly does this dog function in war conditions?"

"That's different. We sleep in the same cot when we're deployed."

The animal had to be seventy pounds, all legs and chest, wedged brown head and speckled all over with flecks of caramel that matched Ethan's eyes. "One cot for the two of you? Crowded much?"

"Nah, unless he's trying to hog the blanket."

Chuckling, she decided not to admit that Baby slept curled at the foot of her bed every night. Ethan's gaze went to the jimmied bedroom window and her humor vanished. Back to grim reality. Someone had been in her borrowed house. Someone who wanted to torture her.

Again her thoughts turned to Andy. Could he have violated his parole already? Somehow found her? He would have known from the trial of Jillian's involvement, perhaps figured Kendra would seek out her old friend. Andy was smart and as focused as a heat-seeking missile.

"Best to loop in the cops," Ethan said.

"I think it's better not to involve them at this point. They're looking into the shooting, that's enough. We don't need to bring them in for a bunch of wasps."

"I say you're wrong. If it's the Andy guy, cops can track him."

"If it's not," she countered, "too much cop involvement will scare away Sullivan."

He didn't answer and she knew she'd touched the right chord. He wanted Sullivan badly, and he wouldn't do anything to jeopardize the capture, even if it meant cozying up to a woman playing the part of his ex-wife.

Do your PI thing. Show him you're working through it, too. "This was elaborate, a lot of work for Andy, if it was him. How was it done?"

"Got to go at a wasp nest at night, when the insects are inactive. There's one hole at the bottom so you don't shine any lights or touch the nest in any way. Raise up a netted bag or something, with a cinch noose around the top, trap everything inside, knock the nest loose. Whoever it was botched the thing. Probably dropped it and retrieved only a small piece of it."

"Good thing for me," Kendra said with a shiver. "If it had to happen at night, it must have been harvested pretty recently or the wasps would be dead."

"Yes, ma'am."

"Probably from somewhere close by."

"Yes, ma'am."

"A lot of work just to freak me out."

"Yes, ma'am."

"Do you have anything else to contribute?"

"No, ma'am."

She huffed. "Will you *please* call me Kendra? If I promise not to tell anyone about your cowardly dog?"

He cocked his head. "I will consider it."

"It'll have to do."

He eyed the small outbuilding crowding one corner of the yard. "Okay to bunk there?"

She started. "What?"

"I should be on the property."

To be her personal bodyguard? "I could have handled the shooter and the wasps myself. I don't need you to—"

He cut her off with a look. "We're supposed to be reconciling, remember? So unless you want me to bunk inside the house…"

She went completely speechless, picturing the tiny home and him sprawled out on the sofa, long limbs draped over the ends, and her skin prickled all over again. It aggravated her that he appeared completely nonchalant, calmly discussing their fake marriage while she had a herd of elephants thundering around in her stomach. How could she send him packing without compromising the case? She realized the silence had gone on too long.

"Right. Of course. Yes."

He strode over to the little mother-in-law unit, Titus right at his heels. Pushing open the door, she peered over his shoulder at a minuscule kitchen that opened onto a cramped bedroom and living room. Ethan had to duck his head to enter. She stood on the doorstep as Titus pushed past her.

"It's kind of small," she said.

"Plenty bigger than a barrack's cot, and I'm not sharing it with a bunch of sweaty guys, so that's a plus."

She realized she was standing close, so close her shoulder grazed his arm. She edged away. "Do you need… I mean, stuff?" Why was her mouth going on without any consultation with her brain? "Uh, clothes and a toothbrush? I think there's a store close by."

He did not seem to notice her babbling.

"Got gear in my truck."

Of course he did. Her aggravation peaked. "Is that

right? So you were planning to stay this whole time, even before you asked me? Isn't that a little presumptuous?"

He didn't exactly smile, but his lips quirked. "Always carry a pack, ma'am," he said. "Never know where you're going to be billeted. Guy's gotta have his creature comforts."

Mortified, her pulse pounding, she figured there was no possible way she could embarrass herself any further. Escape was the only answer. "Great. I guess you're all set then."

"One thing, though. Mind if I get myself some water and maybe a PB and J? I saw creamy peanut butter in the pantry. Not as good as crunchy, but I can make do. I'm tough that way."

"Still hungry?"

"Always hungry, ma'am. Mama says I was born famished and it seems the condition has stuck." His caramel eyes were soft, sparkling with humor and sincerity. Ethan Webb was confounding, a mixture of cocky and kind, altruistic and chauvinistic, frivolous and ferocious, as if he would fit right on the screen of an old Western one moment and a military thriller the next. It was a heady mix. In short, Ethan Webb made her nervous.

"Help yourself," she managed.

"Okay. I'll fix my sandwich, then you can lock up behind me."

Titus sneaked around Ethan, and in one long jump he was settled in the bed, eyeing his partner as if to say, "I'm tired. Isn't it bedtime yet?"

"You better tell your dog it's not quite time for lights out."

"I could tell him," Ethan said, shaking his head at his hopeful companion, "but I don't think he's gonna believe me."

* * *

Ethan slept as he always did, like the proverbial log. He awoke at his customary 0500, ready for a sunrise run with Titus, the scent of cinnamon floating through his memory. He really had unsettled her and the thought made him smile for some reason.

A couple of miles would both allow him to stretch out his legs and familiarize himself with the neighborhood. He and Jillian had lived in a roomy apartment closer to Canyon when they'd been married. Somehow it made him feel better that Kendra wasn't staying in a house where he and Jillian had lived together, battled each other, and where his marriage had exploded into great big messy shrapnel.

The house was still dark and he didn't figure most civilian women would be up until sunrise. He set off on his run, Titus at his heels, past Mindy Zeppler's house just as the sky was shifting from black to gray. He was comforted to know there was a good deal of brush-filled space between her property and Jillian's rental, which meant she would not see Ethan coming and going from the mother-in-law unit. It'd be tough to explain that one.

The street was tree-lined and wide in the way of older developments, and the fresh morning air took him back to his boyhood in Tennessee. Long lazy summers when he and his brother, Luke, sneaked out to go fishing without waking his parents. He could practically taste the squashed sandwiches they'd thrown in their packs, which they'd wash down with warm water. The friendly competition between them led to good-natured wrestling and occasionally a few half-hearted punches. Man, how he missed his brother. Landon Martelli, the K-9 trainer at Canyon, had been the closest he'd ever come to someone besides Luke. He quickened his pace, feet pounding over the pavement.

Gonna get you justice, Landon. Gonna bring down Boyd Sullivan.

A car pulled up next to him.

"Did your dog sleep well?" Kendra wore a baseball cap, her hair peeking out from under it.

He stopped so quickly that Titus thunked into his shin and let out a bark of displeasure before he turned his nose toward the stopped car.

"What are you doing out by yourself?" Ethan snapped.

"I took a cab to the all-night rental car place and got myself a loaner. Then I worked out at the gym before I did some internet business at the cafe."

So much for his theory that she'd been asleep. A bone-head move and a dangerous one, in his opinion. "That is not a good idea," he managed. "Going out on your own under the present circumstances."

She waved him off. "I was in public places the whole time."

"At this hour, how many people are around? Besides, it doesn't matter." He lowered his voice and forced a smile as a lone jogger neared. Keeping the smile plastered in place, he bent to her window. "Someone is trying to kill you and they're not missing by much." The man jogged closer. "Honey," he added.

"Well, darling," she said as she gave him a saccharine smile, "I have a job to do and you're not my boss, so don't talk to me like one."

"I wasn't," he said, waving at the runner who offered a friendly nod as he went past.

"Yes, you were." She was still smiling. "But I brought you some breakfast, pumpkin. A nice muffin."

Pumpkin? Glowering, he snatched the bag from her fingertips. "Thank you."

"No problem, pumpkin. See you back at the house."

She left him there on the sidewalk, holding the bag, grumbling to his dog.

"Pumpkin?" Was that payback for the kiss?

Titus flapped his ears.

Suddenly he did not feel quite so much like he had the upper hand anymore. "This situation is getting a mite tangled."

Titus sniffed the bag, swiped a tongue around his lips and turned back toward home.

Ethan walked behind, cooling down physically and mentally on the way back. In the kitchen, he found Kendra scribbling on a notepad, a phone pressed to her ear. A pot of coffee steamed on the counter. She waved to him to help himself while she finished her call. He was through his first cup of coffee and half the muffin when she disconnected.

"The dead marine—the one Sullivan killed. I was just getting some backstory on that. The man was assigned to the mess hall, custodial duty mostly. His uniform and ID were taken, of course."

She was suddenly all business. Okay, he would take his cue from her tone. "Sullivan's in the area, no doubt about it. Close. Could be your former boyfriend is, too. He made his last parole appointment, but that was Tuesday morning. Could have made it here in time to wrestle up the wasp nest."

She stared at him. "You've been investigating?"

"Affirmative. Need to know which threats are coming from where."

"We are working on catching Sullivan. Andy is my problem."

He put down his coffee cup. "Until the threats against you end, it's our problem."

Pink flushed her cheeks. "There is no 'our.' Andy is a separate investigation, mine only. When it comes to him, we're just...sharing air space."

He laughed, and slapped a hand on the table. "Good one."

"I wasn't trying to be funny."

He shook his head. She was so different than his ex wife, in spite of the resemblance. "Sorry, you have these really cute facial expressions when you're irate, but like it or not, we're partners until Sullivan is brought down and any baggage you bring to the case is relevant to that end."

"Baggage?" She stood suddenly, giving him her back and staring out the window.

He rubbed a hand across his brow and pushed away from the table. "I shouldn't have said that. You got a painful past with this guy, and I didn't mean to be callous about it." He reached out, her shoulder delicate to the touch. "Insert dumb foot into fat mouth."

She didn't react for a moment and he was about to take his hand away when she finally spoke.

"I deserved what I got with Andy," she murmured.

There was a river of anguish in that last statement. "You made mistakes."

"Big ones. Drinking too much, pills. Anything to make him—" She stopped.

Love me, Ethan finished silently. He knew what that was like, turning yourself into something you weren't in order to be loved. He could write a book on the subject. "You survived," he said softly, kneading her delicate shoulder. "You learned."

"God saved me from Andy by bringing Jillian into the picture at just the right moment. To this day it surprises me that I even sent her that text. She'd called me the day before to tell me she was in the area visiting a cousin and could we meet up. I blew her off. To be honest, I was ashamed for her to see me the way I was. I was so different in prep school when we were roomies." She sighed. "Fast-forward to age twenty-two and I'm up to my ears in alcohol and an abusive relationship. I didn't want anyone to see me like that, but when I finally figured out what Andy planned to do…"

"Hold up the convenience store?"

She turned and his hands fell away. Something like betrayal flickered through her eyes. "I forgot. You're a military cop. You already know all about my past, don't you? Why am I going on about it?"

"I know some of the facts, not the reasons behind them."

"What does that matter? I did terrible things and Jillian saved me from myself. That night, the night of the holdup, I called her and she came and got me while he was away, bundled up my stuff and drove me out of town. Andy went through with his plans anyway, got caught and he went to prison. I…I started going to church after that. But now I'm in deeper trouble than I ever was. Paying the price, I guess. I earned that."

"No condemnation, not anymore. God's forgiven you, if you've asked Him to."

She turned those eyes to him, warm and damp with suppressed tears. Then she looked down as if ashamed, but he crooked his finger under her chin and gently eased it up. "The past is in the rearview. It brought you where you are, but you can't drive if you're too busy looking backward."

A tiny sliver of a smile quirked the corner of her lips, his reward.

After a moment, she nodded and stepped away.

He found he wanted to do more, to show her with an embrace that he understood, that he could relate. There'd been plenty of shipwrecks in his own life, his marriage to Jillian being the worst. He prayed he would forget about her, but to date, he had not prayed he could forgive her. Maybe he never would.

So free with spiritual advice, aren't you, Ethan? his conscience taunted. *Not lookin' at the mess with Jillian in your own rearview mirror?*

His phone buzzed with a reminder. "I have to go back to Canyon today to meet with the team about Sullivan."

"I'll stay here and keep digging."

"Uh-uh. You should be with me. Team should know what's going on."

She screwed up her mouth. "Want to tell the truth? You're afraid I'll do something reckless if left unattended, aren't you?"

"No, ma'am, but all the horses in this team need to be pulling in the same direction."

"More Tennessee wisdom?"

"If the saddle fits…" He drained his coffee. "I'm just… concerned about your safety. Sullivan murdered a cook and stole his ID to get onto base at Canyon, but someone's helped him."

"And now he's got a uniform and ID from the soldier he murdered at Baylor so he's got access to the US Marine base also. You're wondering if he's got an accomplice here, too."

Ethan nodded. "He always seems to be one step ahead of us."

"So maybe you've got a leak inside your investigation team."

Ethan washed his mug in the sink to avoid answering. He was not sure how much of the team's work to share with her. "Just keep your eyes peeled, okay?" His phone buzzed again. "And Marine battle dress will do. I assume Jillian left some for you."

She nodded and he checked his phone. A text from his pal Linc. You and Jillian patch things up?

Had the Canyon team heard of his undercover assignment so quickly? It was supposed to be kept on a need-to-know basis. He texted back. Where'd you hear that?

Before Tech Sergeant Linc Colson replied, he got a second message from a friend who rented the apartment next to him at Canyon.

Dude, madly in love with your ex?

Ethan was texting furiously when Linc sent him the source, a link to an anonymous blog that had cropped up recently and attracted dedicated followers on and off the base.

The first line made charges detonate all along his spine.

> *"Rumor has it that Ethan Webb is still madly in love with his ex-wife Jillian Masters and he's been making the long drive between Canyon and Baylor on a regular basis. Completely smitten, he's spending every moment with her, desperate to win her back. Will we hear wedding bells ringing out again for these two? Or is it all a ploy to help catch the Red Rose Killer?"*

He stopped reading, smacking the phone down on the table.

Kendra eyed him along with Titus. "Bad news?"

"When we get to Canyon, I'm going to have to make a side trip," he said through gritted teeth.

SIX

Kendra pulled on the baggy military pants, top and boots, gathering her hair into a tight twist and pinning it under the cap. Jillian was taller but no one would notice the extra length tucked into her boot tops. Baby sat on the bed and watched her.

"How'd I get to be a marine, Baby?" Kendra mused. "A naval aviator yet. I wouldn't have even survived boot camp." *And you might not survive this.* She tucked a small tape recorder in one pocket and locked her weapon in the gun safe Jillian had in the closet. There was no way she was getting through air force security with a Glock strapped to her side. Besides, a pilot would not carry a weapon unless on a mission. Was Sullivan hiding out on Canyon Air Force Base? Or was he right here near Baylor, enjoying toying with her until he was done playing?

She cuddled Baby, kissed her head and made sure the house was secure and the new lock Ethan had installed on the bedroom window firmly fastened before she went to meet Ethan and Titus at his truck.

If she wasn't mistaken, Ethan seemed to jump when he saw her, an involuntary jerk, before he looked down at his boots. His own airman battle uniform were of a darker palette than hers, the Security Forces blue beret snug on his head. Hastily, she scanned her uniform. "Did I get something wrong?"

"No, uh, you just…" He shook his head and gestured to the driver's-side door, which he had already opened. "Let's get rolling."

By the time the seat belt was buckled, she'd figured it out. Sometimes she forgot she was the spitting image of his ex-wife. He stared out the window, jaw tight, guiding the truck back to Canyon. What had Jillian done to him?

Best for you not to know. Just get the job done.

Titus whined from the space behind the driver's seat.

"Doesn't like riding in the back," Ethan explained.

"Sorry, dog," Kendra said. "Get over it. You're not the boss of me."

Ethan laughed, and she felt relieved to see the tension drain away. "Got two older sisters I wish I could convince of that. They live in Tennessee and every time I go home they have a bunch of women they want me to meet." He sighed. "They figure every man who isn't married surely should be working toward that end."

She chuckled. "I always wanted a sister. I guess Jillian was the closest I ever got."

"No siblings?"

"One brother. We're not close anymore."

"Why not?" He grimaced. "Oh, wait. Was that a nosy question?"

"Yes."

"That mean you aren't gonna answer it?"

Another back seat whine from Titus.

"When I started hanging around with Andy, my brother, Kevin, told me to break it off, that Andy was bad news. I didn't want to hear it. The deeper I got into trouble, the more I shut Kevin out until he washed his hands of me. I don't blame him really. My mother was an addict with mental problems, but Kev worked really hard not to repeat the pattern, to make a life for him and his wife and their baby." She cleared her throat. "I wouldn't have wanted me around them, either."

"Have you contacted them since?"

"Since I got clean? No. The farther away from them I am, the farther away Andy is." The remnant of the wasp sting on her cheek throbbed a reminder.

The long drive to Canyon Air Force Base finally ended. The road leading to the security gate was lined in barbed wire, until finally they got to an armed MP with a rottweiler tethered to his wrist. Ethan rolled down his window, and Titus issued a friendly bark, trying to jam his snout out the gap until Ethan backed him off. The rottweiler wagged his hind end in greeting.

"Ethan," the MP said after saluting. "Good to see you."

"Hey, Linc. Reporting for the meeting."

Linc's eyes shifted to the passenger seat. "Ma'am," he said bobbing his chin at her. His eyes were hard and flat, his mouth tight. Clearly he was no fan of Jillian Masters. She kept her cap pulled down.

Linc inspected the car and his dog sniffed every inch of the vehicle also.

"He's your friend?" Kendra whispered.

"Security's buttoned up since the killings. Linc's gonna do his job, whether we're pals or not."

When they were waved through, Kendra figured it was time to ask. "Who's on your list of suspects for Sullivan's accomplice?"

He hesitated. "That's a need-to-know basis."

"That's perfect, since I need to know." She could see him weighing it, measuring his trust in her.

He exhaled. "A few of the women he's dated. We've done initial interviews."

"No. I mean insiders, people on base or near it."

Again, silence.

"As you pointed out, I painted a target on my back."

More silence.

She grabbed his forearm, earning a growl from Titus. "Do you want to see my PI license? I'm not the enemy and I deserve to know. What's that you said about horses pulling in the same direction?"

He rubbed a hand over his face. "Man, I hate when my words are used against me."

She sat back with a victory smile. "So let's hear it."

Ethan fiddled with his beret. Fiddling? He wasn't a fiddler and he didn't want to tell her or anyone about the case. But he'd done a little checking on his own. She was a good PI, top-notch as a matter of fact, with plenty of cases solved and some with nasty connections to drug trafficking and murder. He figured she had a right to know.

"Three top the list at the moment. Rusty Morton, a buddy of Sullivan's, who works at the K-9 training center, but I'm having doubts. Second is Jim Ahern, flight mechanic."

"Who else?"

"A nurse on base here, Vanessa Gomez. She treated Sullivan after a fight, but she's gotten a rose so we initially struck her from the list."

"Initially?"

"Jillian was always jealous of Vanessa after she treated me for an injury. Accused her of flirting with me. Jillian always maintained Vanessa sent the rose to herself to throw us off the scent."

"But you don't believe it?"

"I don't believe anyone anymore. We got more suspects than Dole has pineapples. We did clear Zoe Sullivan, his half sister. Boyd's got a soft spot for her, but she's not assisting him. She's Linc's wife now and they're raising her son, Freddy, together." No need to go into the whole hair-raising story about Zoe's near-death experience from which Linc helped her escape. Linc, Zoe and Freddy were a family, and Ethan was pleased that at least one good thing had come out of the Sullivan mess.

"Anyone else?"

"Yvette Crenville, a nutritionist, dated him but they busted up pretty publicly when Sullivan was dishonorably discharged. That was the tip of the iceberg of course, since he was later imprisoned for a killing spree that left five people dead."

"Do you trust her?"

"Like I said…" He got out of the car in front of the base news office, and she did the same. Tension rolled off him like storm clouds. "It would be better if you stayed in the truck."

"Would Jillian meekly do what you ordered?"

"I…" His mouth snapped shut. "No."

She gestured. "After you, then." She added, low and soft, "Pumpkin."

Titus licked her hand as Ethan snapped on his leash before they strode into the office. Just before they entered, a man leaning against a trash can caught her eye. He wore clothes that matched hers—a marine, the markings indicating he was a combat pilot like Jillian. The brim of his cap shaded his face, but he was tall, strong, and she had a feeling he was staring right at her.

Muscles in her stomach tensed, deep down. She stared right back at him. Ethan noticed her look. He took a step toward her and the man turned away, heading in the opposite direction.

"Know him?" Ethan said.

"No. You?"

"No. We get marines in here all the time."

Or people who had stolen Marine uniforms and credentials?

Suppressing a shiver, she followed Ethan into the news office.

Ethan did not waste time approaching one particular desk, where a middle-aged soldier with horn-rimmed glasses was tapping away on his keyboard. The name placard on his desk read Captain John Robinson.

Ethan fired off a hasty salute. "The blog. Is it your handiwork, sir?" he said without preamble.

Robinson paused, fingers still on the keyboard until he returned the salute. "Hello, Ethan." He glanced at Kendra and quirked a smile. "Ma'am."

Ethan's shoulders lifted in a tense wall. "All this... drivel about love and whatnot."

Kendra felt her own cheeks heating up. Talk about awkward. She'd not realized until then how difficult it would be for Ethan to pretend to be reconciled and back in love with a woman whom in reality he couldn't stand.

"What's the matter?" Robinson said. "Don't like having your love life splashed over cyberspace?"

Ethan went still, the anger radiating out of him like a solar flare. "Sir, this underground blog has been leaking info that only the investigation team should know. How is that happening? You're the base news reporter. Answer the question, please."

"Well," Robinson said, lacing his fingers together and cradling the back of his head with his outstretched arms. "The answer is... I have no answer, only a theory."

"What theory?" Ethan growled.

"That it's someone close." He turned slowly to the female lieutenant at the next desk, a blonde with blue eyes accentuated by dark-framed glasses. "Someone who felt slighted that he or she didn't get assigned the Red Rose Killer story. Someone who understands websites and is within earshot of all kinds of juicy tidbits both on base and off."

The woman whose placard read Lieutenant Heidi Jenks stood, chin up, and walked right to Robinson's desk. "At least do me the courtesy of not talking about me while I'm sitting five feet away." She squared off with Ethan. "I have nothing to do with that underground blog. Yes, I wanted the Sullivan story and yes," she added, her nostrils flared, "I could do a much better job on it than Robinson here, but I am a journalist, not a gossip columnist."

She fired a look at Kendra. "Personally, I'd be glad if you and Ethan are back together. Marriage vows are supposed to be forever, right?" Her eyes narrowed. "No matter what?"

Time to act the part.

"That's right," Kendra said, keeping her voice even in that flat way Jillian kept hers, which she'd come to admire.

"Then again, some things are hard to forgive. You sure know how to humiliate a man," Heidi said in a low voice only Kendra could hear.

Kendra stared her down. "If you've got something to say, spill it."

"I was just thinking how you embarrassed Boyd Sullivan that day when you were observing the K-9 demonstration here on base and his dog wouldn't perform. It was right before he washed out, remember? You verbally annihilated him in front of everyone. The look on his face was painful to see."

"Are you sympathizing with Sullivan?" Kendra said. "Maybe you feel like he didn't deserve a prison term? Maybe you helped him out after he escaped?"

Heidi's eyes turned stone-hard, her silent pause taut as a steel wire. "No," she said after a moment. "Just wondering if you'd had any more threats against you."

Wasps. A shooting. A guy eyeing her like a mouse in the snake pit. Threats? "Nothing I can't handle, but thanks for your concern."

"Watch your back," Heidi said.

"Is that a warning or a threat?"

Heidi said nothing. She merely stalked from the room.

Kendra felt like she'd just made another enemy. Two minutes flat. A record, even for the woman she was impersonating.

Captain Justin Blackwood rubbed his tired eyes, waving Ethan and Kendra into chairs as he disconnected the phone. "Teenage daughters," he said with a sigh, "are more volatile than gasoline."

"Yes, sir," Ethan said. He'd heard the stories about the captain's daughter, Portia, and he sympathized with Blackwood.

Kendra sat next to him in a row of desks and Titus sprawled on the floor, soaking up the coolness of the tile. Since Linc was on gate duty and FBI Agent Oliver Davidson and Office of Special Investigations Agent Ian Steffan were absent, the team consisted of newlyweds Master Sergeant Westley James, along with his German shepherd, Dakota, his wife, Felicity, and Senior Airman Ava Esposito with her dog, Roscoe. They sat facing Blackwood, who perched on the edge of a table in front of an enormous white board.

Westley wriggled his eyebrows at Ethan. "You've been

a busy boy." He shifted his gaze to Kendra. "Congratulations on your reunion, ma'am."

"So sweet," Felicity said, "only she's not Jillian."

Ethan started and Westley looked from his wife to Kendra. "What...?"

"She's shorter and Jillian doesn't have a dimple, not to mention the fact that Jillian would have already started chatting you up, Westley. She can't help flirting with handsome men, married or not."

Kendra sighed. "It's hard to fool a woman. I'm Kendra Bell." She explained her credentials and the plan with Colonel Masters.

"Harebrained scheme if you ask me," Felicity said. "Any progress?"

"I've been shot at, driven off the road and stung by a nest of wasps. Does that count as progress?"

Westley whistled. "Well, you've stirred someone up, that's for sure."

Captain Blackwood called the meeting to order then. After a brief preamble, he questioned his team. "Where are we in the investigation?"

"Nowhere," Esposito said. "Roscoe and I have been searching all over this area and I've seen no sign of Sullivan, or any more of the missing German shepherds, for that matter, though we did retrieve three other dogs in the last twenty-four hours."

"She's referring to the dogs that Sullivan let out the night he killed Landon Martelli," Ethan explained to Kendra. The knot in Ethan's gut tightened when he said his friend's name aloud. He cleared his throat. "The German shepherds are highly trained canines, the elite. I can't imagine them bolting, yet we still haven't found them."

"It's bizarre," Esposito said, "but that's a small point compared to finding Sullivan."

"Sullivan's accomplice is clever," Blackwood said. "Covering tracks as fast as the guy makes them."

"Linc's looking at the prison records again," Westley said. "Going over the visitor list. We must have missed something."

Blackwood stepped away to take a phone call. When he returned, his expression was hardened into the military mask that meant bad news was coming. The room went quiet.

"A witness who saw the killer leaving the scene of the Baylor marine murder gave police enough for a sketch." He turned his phone around to show them.

The air seemed to leak out of the room as they stared into the drawn face of Boyd Sullivan.

"He's been spotted at a corner store as well, this morning," Blackwood added.

He looked at Kendra. "So it's confirmed, then. Looks like Sullivan is in your neck of the woods now, at least for the moment."

How long would he stick around? Ethan mused.

Until "Jillian Masters," aka Kendra Bell, is dead, his gut told him.

Ethan ground his teeth in frustration as they hit the road back to Baylor. Now they had proof that Sullivan was zeroing in on Baylor and the woman he thought was Jillian.

Beside him, Kendra spoke. "Can you stop there?" She pointed to a gas station. "I have to use the bathroom."

He pulled in, letting Titus out to stretch his legs in the shade of some trees. A couple of kids eyed Titus as kids always did, but their mother pulled them back. Ethan was grateful. Military dogs were not pets, they were warriors, always poised for battle. Titus could be playful and loved kids, but now was not the time. The stakes were too high.

Titus stopped mid sniff, head cocked.

"What is it, boy?"

Ethan saw nothing that would upset the dog, but he knew that Titus had an arsenal of sensory detectors that far surpassed anything Ethan could muster. He moved closer, leaving Titus enough room to orient himself, and waited to see what the dog would show him.

Ethan's blood began to pound as Titus gave a little agitated shake of the head, a sign that meant there was trouble ahead.

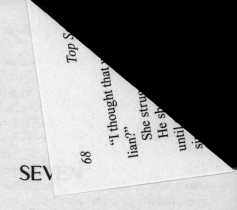

SEV

K endra stepped from the bathroom into the alley, heading toward the truck. A soft sound stopped her. The scuff of a shoe against the cement? The whisk of a shirtsleeve skimming the brick wall? Tiny hairs along the back of her neck prickled. She reached for the gun at her side that wasn't there.

Turning in a quick circle, she saw no one.

"Ninny," she told herself. Paranoia, pure and simple. *Don't let Andy and Sullivan inside your head.*

Continuing down the alley, she picked up her pace, passing a pile of stacked pallets. In a blur, a hand reached out and grabbed her arm, twisting it behind her, and she was shoved against the wall, her cheek jammed to the rough brick.

Heart thundering, she jabbed out an elbow, catching her assailant in the neck, but it set him back only long enough for her to whirl around and face him. His grip on her arm remained, tightened, and he forced her back until her head banged against the wall. It took a moment for her to place him. The tall man, the pilot, dressed in Marine fatigues, the one who'd been watching her at Canyon. His eyes flared with rage.

was you. What are you playing at, Jil-

ggled in his grip. "Let go of me."

ook her until her teeth clacked together. "Not
you give me some answers. I've been trailing you
ce I saw you at Canyon."

"I'm not giving you anything," she gasped. The fingers of his other hand tightened the collar of her uniform into a ligature around her neck. She tried to claw at his eyes, but his grip prevented it.

He pressed close. "We were taking a break while you got your head together, remember? That's what you told me. Now I hear you're back with your ex? The happy couple?"

Her mind struggled to put it together. "Stop..."

He leaned close, his mouth to her ear. "You're not going to toss me out like a piece of garbage, do you understand me? We had a good thing going and you're not going to throw it away for that straight-laced hick of a dog trainer. Do you hear me, Jillian?"

He punctuated each word with a tightening of his grip. Her vision blurred and she knew she had to make a move to prevent him from choking her. Before he could track the movement, she shoved her free hand up through the circle of his arms and jabbed her rigid fingers into his neck near the throat. Gagging, he reeled back and she sagged against the brick, struggling to get her feet to cooperate to flee.

There was a sound of scrabbling paws, a thunderous growl that echoed in the alley as Titus exploded into view and leaped onto the man's back. Kendra panted in relief.

The man roared as the dog bit at his back, tearing sections of uniform away.

"Release," Ethan thundered.

Immediately the dog let go with a howl of displeasure, furry body still quivering.

Ethan trained his sidearm on the fallen man and eyed Kendra. "You okay?"

She nodded, breathless.

"Get up," Ethan ordered her assailant. "Hands behind your head."

The man climbed to his feet. He moved too quickly and Titus stood, teeth bared, barking so loud it made Kendra's ears ring. Ethan silenced the dog.

"Slowly," Ethan advised. "Just so you know, the only thing keeping this dog from tearing you to pieces is me, so I suggest you stand still, very still, and tell me what I want to know."

The man glared.

"Name?"

After a nervous glance at the dog, he said, "Captain Bill Madding."

"You a marine, or just playing dress up for the day?"

His mouth pinched. "I'm a naval aviator. I fly Cobra helicopters while you play around with dogs."

"Yeah? A hotshot pilot and you still got plenty of time to accost women?"

Madding shook his head, his arms dropping until Titus growled, when he raised them again. "I was mad. Hearing that she's back together with you. I mean…" He drilled her with his eyes again, searching, and she saw the moment realization dawned. He peered closer.

"Wait a minute," he said. "You're not Jillian. Who are you?"

Kendra pushed to her feet, willing her lungs back into a normal breathing pattern. "How do you know Jillian?"

He blinked. "I… We went to flight school together. We're colleagues."

"You're more than that," she said.

He pressed his lips together.

She brushed the grit off her arms. "If you don't want to be brought up on assault charges and lose your wings, you better start talking."

He swallowed. "Jillian and I are in a relationship, a serious one, have been for years. She wanted to ease off until after my divorce was drawn up, but when it was done, we got back on track."

Kendra sneaked a look at Ethan. Disgust shone on his face. "So you were having an affair with Jillian while you were still married?"

"My marriage had been over for a long time."

"You still had a piece of paper, didn't you?" Ethan snapped, his drawl thickening. "That's a vow before God, or doesn't that mean anything to you?" Titus stiffened, whining at Ethan's intensity, but Ethan holstered his gun and calmed the dog with a pat. "I guess it means about as much to you as it did to her." He shook his head. "Never mind. I'm calling your Marine cops. They can sort you out."

"No," he said. "Don't do that. Look, I'm sorry I went at you," he said to Kendra. "It was stupid and impulsive. I apologize. I'm set to deploy in a few days and I'll be gone for seven months. I won't be any trouble to you or Jillian."

Ethan's eyes blazed. "No way, Marine. You had your hands around her throat, hotshot. You need some prison time to consider the error of your ways."

Madding's expression went from desperate to something craftier. He arched an eyebrow at Kendra. "Okay. Turn me in and I tell everyone who will listen that you're impersonating Jillian Masters. How's that going to help your investigation, huh?"

Ethan's shoulders tensed. "You're not gonna black-mail—"

"He's right," Kendra said. "Let him go."

"No," Ethan breathed, his ire now burning at her. "No way. He doesn't deserve it."

She walked to him, talking in a low voice. "Ethan, he can end this investigation by blabbing what he knows. Let him go. This isn't related to the Sullivan case."

Ethan looked at the ground and then blew out a long slow breath, his hands fisted on his hips.

"I guess I'll be on my way then." Madding straightened his rumpled uniform. "I don't know what you're working on, but Jillian Masters has stirred up plenty of hornet's nests around here."

Her breath caught. "Did you decide to teach her a lesson by leaving the wasp nest at her house?"

His expression was blank. "I don't know what you're talking about. I hate bugs and that would be a waste of time anyway. Jillian's not scared of anyone or anything on this planet."

But she'd agreed to go into hiding, Kendra thought, so Madding did not know Jillian Masters as well as he thought.

With a loud hiss of breath, Ethan about-faced and called to Titus to follow. The dog did as he was told. "If I ever see you assault a woman again," Ethan called over his shoulder to Madding, "the dog gets his way."

They escorted Madding to the parking lot and watched him get into his car. When they did the same Kendra took time to calm her still jittery nerves. Madding's rough hands brought back memories of Andy. She tugged at the collar of her uniform.

"Sure you're okay?" Ethan said.

"Yeah. I had it under control, but thanks for the assist."

Ethan glowered. "I should have spotted him tailing us. Rookie mistake. I won't make it again."

Back in the truck, Titus swabbed the back of her neck until she batted him away. "What's up with you, dog? I thought he didn't like me."

"You're growing on him."

And Titus was growing on her, too, the seventy-pound goofy bundle of ferociousness and loyalty. "Thanks," she whispered to the dog, "for having my back."

Ethan's brow furrowed and his grip on the steering wheel was unrelenting. He drove fast, too fast. She wanted to say something to break the awkward silence, but she couldn't come up with a single thing. She noticed for the first time a rolled-up scarf at her feet, with dark purple thread and fringe at the ends. "Spiffy scarf."

He shifted on the seat, running a palm over his crew cut. "Yeah, uh, my mom knits them for me. When I deploy I make sure to take a picture of me wearing it and send it to her. She thinks I'll be cold, even though I've tried to tell her it's 120 degrees on a daily basis in Afghanistan. Guys razzed me plenty when they found me taking that picture."

Kendra stifled a chuckle. Did he know how blessed he was to have a mother like that? She looked at his strong profile and decided that he did. After all, he was a man who risked his buddies' ridicule to please his mother. "You're a good son."

"She struggled when my brother died. Deserves a little extra TLC."

His brother. She wanted to ask, but now he was fiddling with the radio, rifling through static and stations. "Don't whine, Titus. Give me a minute. He's particular about his music, that dog. Turn on rap and he'll tear the car apart."

He settled on a slow country tune and Titus risked one more lick to the back of her neck before he settled down in the small space behind the driver's seat for a nap. The miles wound by and Ethan was silent. Okay, if she was going to get to know her enigmatic partner any deeper, it would be on her to make it happen.

"Ethan, does it…did it bother you to hear Madding talk about cheating on his wife with Jillian?"

He drummed on the steering wheel. "Reminded me of the betrayal. That hurt worse than a bullet for a long time."

"I get that. When you realize the person you loved isn't who you thought they were." Andy had been so charming when he wanted to be, but that wasn't who he really was.

"Yeah. Makes me some kind of crazy to have agreed to this charade with her father, huh?"

Not crazy, Kendra thought as she caught the pained twist of his mouth. Ferocious and loyal.

She reached out and grazed his forearm with her fingertips. "Thanks again for what you did back there."

He shrugged and shot her a cocky grin. "See? Told you we gotta be together on this investigation. And you thought I was only good for making frittatas."

She laughed. Just like his dog, Ethan was growing on her, too.

EIGHT

Ethan took Titus out into the woods behind Jillian's rented house that evening as the sun continued its descent. Kendra joined him, rolling her neck, relishing the cooler temperature and the sweet smell of sun-warmed grass, a welcome relief from the case that grew more puzzling with each passing day. "I've been on the phone with Colonel Masters. He wanted to know about our progress. He's anxious."

Ethan snapped a long lead on Titus. "He should be. He lost a marine and he's got people like Bill Madding working for him."

"Masters wants me to report to his office tomorrow for a briefing."

"We'll be ready." He shook his head. "Yeah, don't even bother with 'I don't need you to come along.' Sullivan's got access to Baylor now and Canyon. You're getting an MP and his dog along whether you like it or not."

She sighed. "Whoever's helping Sullivan is doing a bang-up job avoiding arrest. Maybe when your people review the list of prison visitors…"

"Already did that once, but it's possible we missed something."

He bent to Titus and ruffled his ears. "All right, boy, ready? Find it."

The dog took off, nose to the ground, tugging on the lead.

"I hope you're not expecting to find a real cadaver."

"Nah. I left a marker with Sigma Pseudo Corpse Scent earlier."

There was no hint of a smile so she figured he wasn't kidding. "There's a fake scent for corpses?"

"Yeah, comes in three kinds: recently dead, decomposed and drowned. Cool, huh?"

"You don't get invited to many parties, do you?"

He laughed. "Easier than getting real cadaver scents, let me tell you. You wouldn't believe the paperwork. I'm just happy the air force is allowing me to cross-train Titus as a cadaver sniffer."

"It was your idea?"

"Yes."

"Why? Don't have enough to do already?"

He stepped over a fallen log. "I want to help people find answers. If you don't, it can destroy their lives." He paused. "When my brother died, it took three weeks to find him. Those days nearly drove our family to madness."

They watched Titus zigzag from shrub to tree trunk.

Ethan scrubbed a hand over his chin, which showed the beginnings of a five o'clock shadow, and looked over at her. "You want to know, but you're too polite to ask, aren't you?"

She sighed. "Yes. Nosy, I suppose."

"Nah. Natural. I'd want to know, too. My brother, Luke, loved backpacking. He was an outdoors fiend. We used to go all the time. The hard kind of traveling with only a backpack, water, a mat for sleeping, couple of protein bars and a fishing line and that's it."

"Sleeping under the stars, huh?"

"Yeah, we ate that stuff up. Anyway, one time he went by himself 'cuz I was in boot camp. Mama told him not to, of course, but Luke was never one to doubt his own abilities and he didn't take direction well." He held up a palm. "You aren't going to say it runs in the family, are you?"

She mimed locking her lips and throwing away the key.

"Luke was perfectly comfortable in every situation unless you put him in a suit and tie. Then he was like a trussed-up chicken." His grin was boyish. "Anyway, while out on this three-day adventure, he went and got himself hurt—busted femur and ribs, head trauma, the coroner told us later. No phone reception so he couldn't have called for help. Search and Rescue did their best, brought in a helicopter and the whole nine yards. I got leave to fly home to assist. It was twenty-two days before they found his body at the bottom of a ravine."

Her heart squeezed. "How terrible."

"We knew after a few days he was dead, Mama and me. He would have hiked out if he was able. But those days, the hours just stretched on and on. Our church family did their best and held us together, but the wait was agonizing, and the wondering was almost unbearable. At one point we had to wrestle with the knowledge that he might never be found. They can't keep searching forever. Resources have to be reassigned to newer cases. Soldiers' families have to wrestle with that, too, the fear that their son or daughter will never be found, especially if they're lost while deployed. I decided that someday, if I could, I would do something about that."

"It's a hard job to be the one who finds the body, isn't it?"

"Hard job, but a privilege. Finding the deceased is the end of hope, but it's also the start of closure and the beginning of healing." He shrugged. "So that's the story. I wanted to be part of that."

The dappled light from the setting sun teased the caramel streaks from his eyes, rich and vibrant. How could Jillian have betrayed him so brutally? "You are a good man, Ethan." She surprised herself by saying it aloud.

He made a funny face. "Aw, Titus is really the star of our operation, but I cook a better fritatta than him."

She laughed.

"Titus shows promise. When he's ready, he'll be able to detect decomposition of bone, body parts, blood and residue scents even if the body is no longer in place. I read about a case where a dog found a body buried twelve feet deep." He looked suddenly uneasy. "Was that more than you wanted to know?"

"No. Just reinforces that dogs are pretty amazing."

"Oh, yeah." Enthusiasm lit his face. "It's like when you walk into a room and smell chili cooking. Well, a dog walks in and smells each ingredient in the pot. They can discriminate odors individually. Awesome, huh?"

His smile was infectious. "Awesome," she agreed.

"We both have a long way to go. Titus isn't fully trained yet and we haven't even started water recovery work. He's not super enthusiastic about waves, which I tell him is pure cowardice on his part." He eyed the dog. "Gonna have to get you some water wings, huh, boy? But like I said, all the other dogs are gonna laugh at you."

Titus stiffened, pulling to the left toward a wide pile of granite boulders.

Ethan groaned. "No, Titus. That's not where we're

headed, buddy. He's still distracted by other things." He put the dog into a sit, earning a whine from the animal. "I know this is new for both of us but you gotta focus." He scratched Titus's muzzle. "Got it together? Okay. Let's do this. Find the package." He shot Kendra a look. "'Package' is nicer than—"

"A body," she finished.

Again Titus beelined to the left, and only Ethan's strength kept him from yanking the leash free.

"Titus," Ethan started to say when a high-pitched scream cut through the air.

Titus switched gears and bolted for the noise, Ethan and Kendra scrambling to catch up.

"Help," the voice called again. A woman's voice.

Kendra could not pinpoint the source as they crashed through the trees. The canopy of branches grew thicker as they pushed deeper into the woods, the shadows, distorting, disorienting.

"Please," came the cry again.

Kendra pushed faster, praying she would not trip over a tree root and break her ankle, but she dared not slow.

Someone was in the woods with them, someone who needed help.

Ethan followed a dirt trail, feet pounding on the earth before he skidded to a halt where the ground gave way to a creek bed some ten feet below them. Titus would have scrambled down immediately if not restrained.

"Sit," Ethan commanded and Titus instantly obeyed, though he was probably chewing Ethan out in his doggy brain.

Kendra, he saw, was peering over the edge, but the water was screened by a thick tangle of shrubbery. "Who's there?" she bellowed.

A voice from below called out, "Please. I need help."

"Wait," he said, but Kendra did not hesitate, plunging down the steep slope, picking her way between the rocks. Biting back a complaint, he followed.

Branches slapped at both of them, the rocks shifting under his boots. As they cleared the bushes, he saw a bicycle lying on its side in the water, rear wheel spinning lazily. Jillian's neighbor, Mindy Zeppler, sat on a rock, wet and shivering, streaks of mud across her forehead and cheek.

Kendra splashed across the creek. "Are you hurt? What happened?"

Mindy pushed a clump of hair from her face, dirty water trailing down her cheek. "Jillian, I'm so grateful you found me. I forgot to bring my phone with me."

Kendra repeated her question.

Mindy took a breath. "I was riding. I love the woods at this time of day, except for the mosquitoes. I crashed and fell. I'm so glad you were here, too." She looked at Ethan. "Training your dog?"

"Yes, ma'am."

He did not see any visible bleeding on Mindy, no bruising apparent under the streaks of mud, but those would surface later. "Did you hit your head?"

"No. I don't think I broke anything, either." She examined her wrist. "I hope not anyway."

"I'll pull your bike out for you," Ethan said, eyeing it. "Doesn't look too badly damaged."

"We'll help you get home," Kendra said. "Do you want us to call an ambulance?"

Mindy shook her head. "I'm okay. I'm sort of a klutz, as my ex-husband would tell you, but this time I had a good excuse." Fear flickered across her face. "I crashed because…" She swallowed. "Because there was a man, here in the woods."

Ethan's gut tightened. "A man?"

She nodded. "I've only lived here for a couple of years and people are always coming and going, so I don't know everyone, but he was acting weird."

"How?" Ethan allowed Titus to poke his nose into the creek.

Mindy took a breath. "He had binoculars and he wore gloves. Way too hot for gloves, isn't it? He was watching something. I didn't know what at the time, but I think I do now."

Ethan's muscles bunched at the base of his spine. "I think I do also."

Kendra's expression told her she'd reached the same conclusion.

The man in the woods had been watching them.

NINE

Kendra swallowed hard. "Can you describe him?"

Mindy frowned. "It all happened so fast… About five-eight maybe? He wore a hat so I couldn't tell his hair color. I didn't get a good look at him because I was busy crashing my bike. But why would someone be watching you, Jillian?"

Kendra tried to rally her thoughts. She could not get into the Red Rose Killer details, but she had to give Mindy something. "I…I have a violent ex-boyfriend. His name is Andy."

Mindy's brows furrowed. "Boyfriend? I thought…" Her gaze traveled to Ethan. "I thought you two were back together."

"Yes, we are. Andy was ancient history."

"He must have a long memory, if he's still coming after you."

You don't know the half of it. "I'll call the police. They can help keep an eye out." Kendra wondered how she was going to explain the particulars to Officer Carpenter and still keep the investigation under wraps. There was no choice. They had to tell the cops about the current attack since it involved a civilian. Andy couldn't be allowed to endanger anyone else but her, if it really was him.

"Can you stand?" Kendra asked her neighbor, offering her an arm.

Mindy took it, her fingers icy on Kendra's skin. "All your wasp stings are healed up," she said, her eyes wandering Kendra's face.

Kendra wished she had a cap to pull down. "Yes. Much better now."

"Do you think the guy with the binoculars was the one who called me looking for you? Maybe this Andy of yours?"

"I'm not sure," Kendra said. "I'll look into it."

With her support, Mindy seemed to gain strength and they crossed the creek. "Wait," she said. "When I rode up and saw him, he sort of jumped. I think he might have dropped his binoculars."

Kendra's spirit surged. Though he'd been wearing gloves, maybe an errant fingerprint survived, which would reveal exactly who was after her.

"On it," Ethan said. He and Titus began scouring the bushes while Kendra helped Mindy back up onto the trail. She heaved a breath and detached herself from Kendra.

"I'm okay, I think. Just banged up. I can make it back to the house."

"I'll go with you. The police will want to talk to all of us."

Mindy walked a few feet before she suddenly halted. "Here. Look."

Before Kendra could stop her, she reached under the shrubs and grabbed the binoculars, holding them triumphantly. "See? I told you he dropped them." She caught Kendra and Ethan's reaction. "What's wrong?"

"You've got your fingerprints on them now," Ethan told her.

Her face fell. "Oh. Sorry. I didn't think of that."

"It's okay," Ethan said. He pulled a plastic bag from his pocket and Mindy dropped the binoculars in, zipping it closed. "The guy probably didn't have time to search for them with you calling for help."

The three walked slowly from the woods, emerging some ten minutes later at the back gate to Mindy's property. Mindy let them into a small house similar to Jillian's, but decorated in light colors with framed photos covering the wall behind the sofa and a deerskin rug on the floor. A wedding picture showed a much younger Mindy, beaming and beribboned in a fluffy wedding dress, holding an elaborate bouquet.

Kendra touched the silver frame. "Pretty picture."

Mindy eased into a chair, holding an ice pack to her knee that Ethan had fetched from her freezer. "Yes. The marriage was a disaster, but I figured since the dress cost a mint I might as well keep that photo up. Are you…" She grimaced as she flexed her knee. "I mean, are you two going to have another ceremony?"

Kendra couldn't come up with a response.

"Sure we are," Ethan said, beaming. "Only this time it's gonna be a proper wedding on the beach with good food, country music and comfortable footwear. My uniform dress shoes were designed by the enemy to torture me, I'm pretty sure." He looked at Kendra. "This time we're gonna get it right, don'tcha think, Jillian?"

Somehow he had come up with the perfect response, as usual. Kendra heaved a silent sigh of relief. "Sure. Why not?"

Mindy giggled. "Sounds romantic."

Actually, it did to Kendra, too. She'd dreamed of a marriage like that, where things were easy and honest, with someone to encourage her in life and faith. She discovered Ethan was smiling at her. For some reason it brought warmth to her cheeks.

After a thirty-minute wait, Officer Carpenter arrived to take their statements. Kendra met him at the curb.

"Ms. Bell?" he said, eyebrow arched.

"There are a few things I need to tell you before you go in there."

"You don't say?"

"Yes, sir."

"Is it possible that you have not been forthcoming with the police?"

"You know who I really am, sir, but I need to tell you who I'm pretending to be and why I need you to keep the pretense going."

He folded his arms across his chest. "You may talk, Ms. Bell, and I will decide what I will or will not do with your information."

"Yes, sir," she said. Blowing out a breath, she plunged in.

Ethan stayed mostly silent as Carpenter finished scribbling down the information, took the binoculars and said good-night to Mindy Zeppler. Ethan, Titus and Kendra walked him to the car. Kendra had told him everything, and apparently he was going to keep her cover intact since he had not revealed Kendra's true identity in front of Mindy.

"I will check on the whereabouts of Andy Bleakman," Officer Carpenter said. "As far as Sullivan goes, I've only got the barebones information that your task force has been willing to share." His tone was bitter, as Ethan's would be if he was being shut out of an investigation.

Ethan had already been forced to share more than he wanted to in the first place. Sullivan was discharged from the air force, and it was their duty, their responsibility, to put him away. "Got anything from the shooting yet?"

The officer shrugged. "Gun wasn't military issue. Rifle, standard Ruger. Plenty of folks around here have them for hunting. Shooter didn't recover his brass at the scene so we've got shell casings. Not the best marksman, in my humble opinion. How about Sullivan? He any good with a rifle?"

"Enough to pass basic training, but he was no sniper, that's for sure."

"What about accomplices?"

Ethan stiffened, watching the officer's body language. "What are you thinking?"

Carpenter shrugged. "Just wondering if he's got a lady friend."

Ethan stared at the cop, assessing him now. "We've got females on the suspect list. Why?" Carpenter was enjoying making them wait, payback for being shut out of the investigation to date.

He thumbed his mustache. "We picked up a partial footprint in the soft dirt near the shell casings. Real small. Looks to be from a woman's shoe."

"You took—"

"Impressions, of course, and when we're good and finished examining them I'll send them along to your people at Canyon."

Ethan didn't argue. It was the best they could do. "Thank you, Officer."

"Don't thank me," he said. "Footprint isn't gonna help much. Likely the binoculars aren't, either, but we'll scan for prints anyway."

They walked back to Jillian's house in silence. The air was thick with the promise of a storm, Texas style. In the kitchen he supplied fresh water for Titus and let him

out in the yard before the rain arrived. Baby crept out
from under the sofa, where she'd streaked the moment
they returned. He leaned on the counter, details pinging
rapid-fire through his mind. Finally he went to the fridge
and opened it, staring inside as if there might be an answer somewhere in there. He sighed. "You want a Coke?"

"Sure."

"What kind?"

She quirked an eyebrow. "Coke is a kind."

"Nah, that's a category. What kind do you want?"

She laughed. "That's a Southern thing, isn't it?"

He returned the smile and handed her a root beer, taking one for himself, too. He had a need to hear her talk,
to soak in the way her face showed her feelings. "Where
you from then where they don't speak properly?"

"I grew up in Colorado. My brother's still there with
his family, but I haven't been to see him since I left for
prep school, only texted a few times. I have a small office clear across the state, closer to where I went to prep
school."

"Where you met Jillian."

"Yeah. I met Jillian on my first day when I transferred
in as a sophomore. I was a charity case. Scholarships paid
for everything. I was surprised that Jillian wanted anything to do with me. I certainly wasn't part of her circle,
her being the daughter of a high-ranking marine. She
had all the money and clothes she wanted while I was
wearing a secondhand uniform and working at the gas
station at night. Jillian was what I wanted to be—smart,
confident, popular. She never had a Saturday night without a guy by her side." She broke off. "Oh, I'm sorry if
that was insensitive."

"Nah. I admired her confidence, too. I was just dumb
enough to think that when we got married, she'd give up

all the other men." He sipped the cold soda, gesturing for her to continue.

"I met Andy when I was eighteen and all my good sense went out the window. I thought he was made for me, the glue for all my broken parts. I never knew my father. My mom had me when she was sixteen, and she had mental problems as far back as I can recall, so I guess I didn't know what real love was supposed to look like."

"It can be tricky to spot," he said. "I'm not sure I know what it would look like, either."

A look, both gentle and poignant, washed over her and he watched, dazzled by it.

"Real love would be two people putting God at the top of the list," she said. "That's all I know. Man and wife are going to disappoint each other at times, but He won't and He's got to be the glue that holds it all together."

He examined the rich mahogany of her eyes, the light dusting of freckles across her nose. In the small circle of overhead light, with her hair loose, swimming in her baggy ABUs, she did not look much like his ex-wife. Certainly not the sincerity that made her so very vulnerable, the honest desire to start over again and start fresh with God at the center. He wanted to keep right on staring at her, memorizing the details of her face, her long fingers, the tiny scar next to her eyebrow, but something achy and tight took hold of his heart and he got up to knock it loose. "I'm going to check the perimeter again, be sure no one tampered with any locks while we were gone."

She nodded. "If that was Sullivan in the woods, he's close."

"Too close."

"Carpenter believes the accomplice is a woman," she said. "Your suspect list included Vanessa Gomez, Zoe

Sullivan, Yvette Crenville and the two women Sullivan dated."

"Linc interviewed one again just recently. I'll call and pick his brain and schedule an interview with the others."

"And you've ruled out Zoe. Vanessa got a rose, though it might have been a diversion." She paused. "There's one more name I was thinking of."

"Spill it."

"The woman at the base news office."

"Heidi Jenks? What would her motive be?"

"I can't imagine, but she has access to information, and you suspect her of being the underground blogger. I think she suspected I wasn't Jillian, the way she looked at me."

"I've learned by now not to toss any theories aside. I'll look into it."

"Me, too. Good night."

Ethan paused at the door. "Storm coming in."

She sighed. "Seems like there's always a storm coming in."

He smiled and put on a hick accent. "Lessen it's a frog strangler, I reckon we'll be okay."

She laughed. "Tell that to your chicken of a dog."

Smiling, Ethan let himself out and waited until she locked the door, the light silhouetting her in gold. Titus wandered over and the two made their way back to the in-law unit. As he pulled off his boots for the night he found his eyes traveling to the window, to the treetops visible just over the fence, shadowed by ominous clouds.

If you're out there, Sullivan, I'm going to find you.

There'd be no more victims.

Especially not Kendra.

TEN

They arrived at Colonel Masters's office and waited outside the door until they were summoned. Ethan looked about as happy as he had the last time they'd been to see Masters. When the aide ushered them in, he brought Titus with them and let him up on one of the chairs.

Kendra gave him a questioning look.

"Masters hates dogs," he whispered.

She smothered a grin at the mischievous gleam in his eye. They entered, and Ethan fired off the obligatory salute.

The colonel did not offer them a seat. "I want to know everything about the hostile in the woods."

"All we know," Kendra said, "is that it was a male that matches Sullivan's description. The police have the binoculars for printing."

"I didn't want police in the picture," he snapped.

"We had no choice," Kendra said. "There was a civilian involved. She could have been hurt."

"We reported all this over the phone," Ethan said. "Why are we here?"

Masters didn't raise his voice, but his tone turned to steel. "Because I sent for you, and you're both working for me."

Ethan's cheeks went scarlet. "You don't—"

"He brought you here because of me," said a voice from the file room. Kendra gasped as Jillian stepped out wearing jeans and a T-shirt. She almost didn't recognize her with her hair dyed a dark brown and her eye color changed to green with the help of some tinted lenses.

Jillian smiled and the women hugged. She nodded at Ethan who was breathing hard, staring at Masters. "You're nuts, bringing her here. If anyone who knows her happens to—"

"You worry too much, Ethan," Jillian said. "Always have."

His eyes sparked fire. "You must be plenty worried, too, to go into hiding and let someone else fight your battles."

Jillian's face settled into an angry mask and she started to retort, but the colonel stopped her with a raised palm.

"Enough. Jillian's here because she wanted an update and she's impatient for results."

"Can you blame me? I want my life back."

"We ran into a friend of yours who wants the same thing," Ethan said. "Bill Madding."

Her lips thinned. "We're over."

Ethan glared. "Funny, he doesn't seem to think so."

"That's personal."

"You were in a relationship with a married guy. He attacked Kendra. That makes it our business."

Jillian folded her arms. "He's divorced now, but he has a wandering eye. I dumped him when I saw the text on his cell phone from someone named Lizzie with all the kissing emojis."

Ethan's tight jaw telegraphed his feelings. Kendra understood. How could Jillian stand there and criticize someone for being unfaithful? It was a case of the plank in the eye blocking out the speck in another's.

Kendra took a subtle step between Jillian and Ethan. "What can you tell us about Madding?"

Jillian sniffed impatiently. "Nothing to tell. He thinks he's a macho man's man, hunts, fishes. It gets old after a while." She waved her hand, as if to push aside that line of questioning. "That's a dead end. Where are we with Sullivan's accomplices?"

"The police suspect it might be a woman," Kendra replied.

"That's not a new theory."

"What do you think about Heidi Jenks?" Kendra asked.

Jillian's eyes narrowed as she considered. "I've always thought she was the one behind the underground blog. She'd be in a good position to help Sullivan, since the press has access to plenty of places on base and off." She tugged on a strand of brown hair. "Motive?"

"Could be she had a secret relationship with him."

Masters raised his voice. "This is all well and good about the accomplice, but I want Sullivan, so we've got to force his hand."

"We're working on it," Ethan said. "We'll keep you apprised of our progress so there's no need to drag us in here again." He took a step toward the door, Titus beside him.

"You're not leaving yet," Masters said.

Kendra's stomach tightened. "Why not?"

"Jillian needs to be seen around the base. I've pulled strings to cover her duties, but she can't simply disappear. To that end, I've scheduled you for an overnight SERE training refresher course."

Jillian started to explain. "SERE is—"

"Survival, Evasion, Resistance and Escape training, I know," Kendra said. "I did my homework before I agreed to impersonate a marine."

"No way," Ethan barked. "She'll be out there in the rough, unprotected."

"Not unprotected. You will go with her," the colonel said smoothly. "I'll set the wheels in motion. It's just one overnight, twelve hours max."

Kendra noticed that Jillian did not look at all surprised by Masters's announcement. She blew out a breath. "You are here to prep me for what to expect at the SERE training so I don't blow my cover, aren't you?"

Jillian didn't respond.

"And you're hoping Sullivan will make a move to kill me during the exercise."

Ethan glared at Jillian and her father. "That's exactly what they're both hoping for."

Jillian took Kendra's hand and squeezed, her smile wide, a pained twist to her brows. "I don't want you to get hurt, Kendra. I just need this to be over. I have to get my life back."

By putting mine at risk? Kendra realized in that moment that Ethan had been correct. Jillian really would be content sacrificing Kendra to save herself. She detached herself from Jillian's grip. "I took the case and I'll see it through. You'll get your life back." *And I will have repaid my debt.* She turned to Masters. "When and where do I report?"

Ethan and Kendra were given the standard gear, except for the substitution of blanks for live ammo, and one hour to return home. Just long enough for Kendra to leave Baby with Mindy.

"I would leave her alone for one night, but she needs medicines," Kendra explained to the neighbor.

"Don't you worry about a thing." Mindy cooed into Baby's neck. "I'll take good care of her. Have fun traipsing with your training, now, you hear?"

"We won't go too far. It's just a twelve-hour trek through the wilderness," Kendra said. Ethan wondered if she was trying more to calm herself or Mindy. She was a tough lady, he knew that for sure, but she had no idea what to expect from SERE training. It was going to be a long night.

"In the woods?" As Mindy stroked Baby, a worried frown appeared on her face. "Where the man was?"

"Farther south," Kendra soothed. "It will be okay. I'll be back in the morning. Shall I wait until a decent hour to retrieve Baby?"

"I'm not an early riser, so that would be good." She gave Ethan a sly look. "You two sure know how to go on some pretty wild dates."

Ethan was annoyed to find himself blushing. Survival training was the furthest thing from fun, he wanted to say, and an even further thing from a date.

Besides, if he was going to take Kendra on a date, he would take her to the best BBQ place in Texas and then maybe for a walk under the stars. He'd show her the constellations and buy her the nicest box of chocolates he could find and a big bunch of tulips. His mama always drummed into him that a classy woman must have chocolates and flowers, fine quality chocolates in shiny boxes, preferably soft centers, for some mysterious reason he'd never understood. Nuts and chews would not do. Deployed or not, every year on Mother's Day that was exactly what he got her, too, his mama, the finest woman he knew.

He imagined handing Kendra a bouquet of tulips, maybe pink, the color her cheeks turned when he teased her. That soft, silky pink of sunsets and shells tossed up on the sand.

He blinked. *Where is your mind?* he chided himself. Planning imaginary dates with Kendra when there was a killer at large? "Time to get going."

The training would begin at Baylor with a refresher, and then they'd move out, traversing the course, which would take them off base and deep into the surrounding woods. Twelve hours in which the twenty some odd soldiers would spread out, conceivably on their own, but he fully intended to break that rule, until they rendezvoused back at base at precisely 0600 hours. Normally he'd relish the situation, the challenge of relying on his wits and savvy, but now he had Kendra to think about. Open spaces and sitting ducks came to mind, and the delicate pink of her cheeks that kept popping into his mind to his dismay.

They reported to the classroom first, where an instructor gave Titus a stern eye but made no remark about Ethan's presence. He'd been given his marching orders from Masters but it didn't mean he had to like them.

"Your job, soldiers, is to survive, evade, resist and escape. If you fail at these endeavors, you will face your enemy armed only with the articles from the Code of Conduct."

He slapped a hand on the poster on the wall and they read the articles aloud.

"I am an American fighting in the forces which guard my country and our way of life. I am prepared to give my life in their defense," Ethan recited.

He sneaked a look at Kendra, small and determined, her chin high and proud in a way that made his stomach tighten. She recited, "I will never surrender of my own free will. If in command, I will never surrender the members of my command while they still have the means to resist."

The room swelled with the words of the dozen men and women. He felt the ripple of pride, as he always did, the privilege of serving shoulder to shoulder with people who meant every word they spoke.

When they reached the last article on the poster, their volume rose together, each syllable crisp and precise.

"I will never forget that I am an American, fighting for freedom, responsible for my actions and dedicated to the principles which made my country free. I will trust in my God and in the United States of America."

Kendra looked at him then. She didn't smile but the courage in her eyes got right inside him.

"Soldiers," the instructor said, sweeping the room and lighting for a moment on Kendra. "Don't get caught."

She won't, Ethan promised silently.

They assembled outside and prepared to load up in the back of a truck.

"Be back here at oh six hundred or you flunk the course," the instructor said.

Kendra crawled up into the truck and Ethan followed, hoisting Titus up behind him.

"Since when are dogs allowed, man?" a young marine said from the corner, a touch of resentment in his tone.

Ethan shot him a grin. "Don't worry. He's not much of an advantage since he's scared of the dark."

That got the chuckles he was looking for.

"How long has it been since your last SERE training, Jillian?"

Ethan's head jerked toward the familiar voice.

Lieutenant Heidi Jenks sat against the truck wall,

wearing the same woodland fatigues, notebook in her hand. The plastic cover was torn, held together with duct tape.

Kendra gaped. "What are you doing here?"

"I was talking to the Baylor base reporter to get some intel on the murder and I heard about this class. I thought it would make for an interesting article," she said as she eyed Ethan, "since one of our own is participating for some reason."

"Planning on putting this up on the underground blog?"

Jenks smiled. "I told you, that isn't me."

"I don't believe you," Ethan said.

She lifted a shoulder. "I'm having trouble believing a few things myself." Her eyes locked on Kendra. "So when exactly was your last SERE training?"

Ethan had to get her off that line of questioning. "So you're going to complete the SERE training with us?"

"Just until sundown when the hunting starts," Jenks said.

"And who gave you permission?"

"Colonel Masters himself."

Ethan bit back a groan.

"Weird, huh?" Jenks lowered her voice to a whisper. "I mean, why would Masters have his daughter participate in SERE when she's got a serial killer gunning for her?"

And why would he let a nosy base reporter tag along?

Same reason.

He wanted to make it easy.

If Heidi Jenks was Sullivan's accomplice, Masters had just invited her to take the kill shot.

ELEVEN

Kendra repeated the instructions to herself.

"Find water. Move toward the rendezvous point while avoiding capture." And Heidi Jenks, she told herself. They had a two-hour grace period before the marines began to hunt them down.

Ethan and Titus were somewhere close by, she knew, but they could not join her with so many other soldiers around. Participants were supposed to go it alone. She suspected Ethan would be breaking that rule early on. She started hiking up river, grateful that her brother, Kevin, had repeatedly dragged her out camping in the mountains. She had a basic idea of how to stay alive, at least for one night. First order of the day was to obtain safe water and fill the empty container in her pack.

Jenks appeared at her elbow. "So you didn't answer my question. How long has it been since you completed your last SERE training?"

The reporter was as determined as a dog on the scent, Kendra thought. She squared off with her. "My sole job right now is to survive and not get captured, so with all due respect, I won't be able to answer your questions. As a matter of fact, I'd like you to leave me alone, period."

To her surprise, the woman laughed. "That's more polite than I would have thought from you, Jillian. You've changed. Is that why you and Ethan are back together? You've turned over a new leaf?"

Kendra's pulse kicked up a notch. This reporter knew Jillian well enough to know that Kendra wasn't acting quite the part. "That's another question I'm not answering," she said, marching purposefully. "Go find someone else to badger, why don't you?"

"I'm used to reluctant subjects. They warm up eventually."

"Not this one."

To her dismay, Jenks trekked right along with her until they were about a mile upstream. Once she collected her supply of water she intended to move to deeper cover to find shelter until she could decide on the best way to evade the marines assigned to capture her. Sullivan, if he was nearby, would most likely not make a move during the daylight with soldiers in the vicinity. Then again, maybe Jenks would attempt to act for him.

She glanced at the reporter. No visible weapon. But that didn't mean she wasn't carrying a gun in her small pack. Keeping Jenks in her line of sight as best she could, she scooped water into the small bowl from her pack and carried it to a flat spot under a thick canopy of trees. The ground was wet but she managed to find some relatively dry twigs. Removing the faro fire starter from her pack, she knelt and began to rub the striker against the block, a trick Ethan had tried to explain during their drive back to Baylor after leaving Baby with Mindy.

A spark dropped into the tinder, eliciting a wisp of smoke. Elated, she blew gently on the pile, but instead of igniting a flame she promptly extinguished it. She slapped a hand to her thigh.

"A little rusty?" Jenks said.

"Everything's too wet," she muttered.

"I'll see if I can find something drier."

Kendra stared. "You're helping?"

"Yeah, 'cuz you're going to share the water with me, right?"

Mutual cooperation, or an excuse to stay close? Kendra kept at the fire starter until her hands were cramped. The stiff breeze left over from the storm both chilled and frustrated her.

Jenks returned. "Nothing much drier than what you've got."

Kendra fastened a hand on Jenks's notebook. "I need that tape."

"What?"

"The tape that's holding your book together. Let's have it."

"But I—"

"You want the water or not?"

Jenks reluctantly peeled away the tape and handed it over. Kendra made a loose ball of it and nestled it on top of the tinder. This time, the spark caught the tape and sent up a respectable flame that ignited the tinder. Fire. Awesome.

Jenks nodded. "I have to admit, I wouldn't have thought of that."

The fire boiled the water and after it cooled, Kendra filled both their bottles. Never had she appreciated clean water more.

"Thank you," Jenks said. She checked her phone. "Uh-oh. I have to go."

"Where?"

She raised an eyebrow. "You think you're the only one with a duty here?"

"What's your duty exactly?"

"Sniffing out a story, just like I said. I have great instincts and something tells me you've got *newsworthy* written all over you."

"I'm just a soldier trying to get through training."

Her eyes narrowed. "Somehow, I doubt that." A few drops of rain began to fall. "Oh, boy. Another storm. Looks like you're in for long night."

Kendra shrugged. "I've had plenty of long nights."

The shadows shifted, painting Jenks's face in eerie stripes of light and dark. "Some nights are longer than others."

Was that a threat? A promise of trouble to come?

Jenks opened her pack and Kendra bolted to her feet. No sense reaching for her weapon as they were not allowed to use live ammo.

She calmed down when Jenks merely stowed the water bottle in her pack and fastened it closed.

The reporter wasted no time. She shouldered the pack and went on her way. "Hope the morning comes quickly."

Kendra waited until Jenks vanished into the trees before she struck out into the woods. The more tree trunks between her and Jenks the better. Wind rattled the leaves, teased prickles on her skin, but it dampened the heat of the day. She kept within earshot of the river to maintain her sense of direction.

As she hiked the clammy ground she thought she heard someone behind her. She stopped and turned. No one. A few yards off a bird shot from the bushes, startled by something. Ethan and Titus were out there somewhere but for the moment, Kendra was totally and completely alone.

Unless there was someone in the shadows, watching and waiting for their moment to strike.

Kendra followed the river and Ethan and Titus trailed her. There was no imminent danger, yet his instincts were poking him like a kid with a sharp stick as he trailed her. Sullivan was at large; he'd murdered a marine not fifteen miles from here. And now Jenks was cozying up?

Titus managed the hike with his typical enthusiasm, finally flopping down in the shade to rest while Ethan boiled water for both of them when Heidi and Kendra stopped to rest. They'd been hiking for a few hours. Technically, they were not allowed cell phones, but since this wasn't official training for him, he'd taken it along. Unfortunately, the farther he delved into the woods, the worse his signal became. Anticipating the problem, he'd strapped on the trusty Timex he'd bought when he delivered pizza as a sixteen-year-old kid to track the time. The thing had seen him through two deployments, not to mention the adventure when he'd tumbled off a mountain bike back home. It was almost five o'clock. His stomach grumbled. Food was the last item on the agenda. A person could live for weeks without anything to eat, but drinking was another matter entirely.

The canopy of branches squeezed out the light, stripping away the warmth. A branch caught his ankle and he tumbled down a steep incline, the breath driven out of him. Titus looked down from the ridge as if to say, "What did you do that for?" He wagged his tail and barked.

Muttering, Ethan climbed laboriously out. "You could have come and helped," he grumbled to Titus. He huffed out a breath when he realized he was no longer within sight of Kendra. She'd moved out during his tumble.

Quickly, he drank again, refilled the bottle for him and Titus and shouldered his pack.

"Time to find Kendra, boy." He pulled her sweater from his pack. Titus sniffed and tongued the fabric before trotting confidently off between the tangles of spiky branches. Titus wasn't a scent dog, but he'd never failed to blow Ethan away with his skills. Trusting his dog, he followed. He wished he had a good scent article for Sullivan. He'd feel a lot safer knowing Titus had Sullivan's essence stored in that amazing nose of his.

But the woods were full of invisible aromas, and Titus took off after one. Ethan prayed it would lead to Kendra.

As the sun set completely, the rain started to come down in sheets. Kendra figured there was no point in putting up the shelter since there would be an "enemy" soldier combing the woods for her in a matter of moments.

She pulled on the dark-patterned poncho that billowed over her with enough room left over to cover her backpack. Sitting in the scant shelter of a rock formation, she tried to pick out a path. The rising darkness cloaked everything in odd shadows, and a wall of clouds obliterated the moon. The only sound she could discern above the crashing rain was the pounding of her own heart. She'd always avoided the darkness, ever since those long-ago nights when Andy would pace in manic circles deep into the night, smoking and drinking with his friends after she'd crawled away to her own room, addled by drugs, filled with self-loathing. Now, she and Baby slept with a small lamp on so when the nightmares came, bringing the self-recrimination, she would sit up and read the little plaque set on the night table.

There is therefore now no condemnation...

She'd been forgiven, washed clean, but sometimes, especially on moonless rainy nights, she still felt the vicious bite of fear. She wondered why Ethan hadn't tried to make contact.

"Get moving," she ordered herself. "You know which way the river is, so follow it." She forced her cold limbs into motion. As she picked her way over slick logs, past dripping trees, something stirred in the brush. She took cover behind a tree, crouching as small as she could manage, her pulse thundering.

A flicker of light shone, small, the soft glow of a cell phone screen. Phones weren't allowed by the SERE participants, but Kendra had one anyway. Useless without a signal. Those playing the enemy had satellite phones, which worked in spite of the terrain. The glow could be a soldier enacting the enemy role. They had privileges the hunted did not.

Someone moved through the bushes five feet to her right, a man in cammies, walking soft-footed with his rifle raised, water dripping from the brim of his hat. He was tall, like every soldier, it seemed. Like Sullivan. Fright roared through her.

Who are you hunting? her mind screamed. If it was Sullivan, it would be a relief to confront him, to finally face the man she'd been hired to capture. But she could not see clearly through the pounding rain.

When he'd moved a safe distance away, she eased up from her hiding place, intending to follow at a safe distance. If it was a marine tracking her, she'd have to head in the other direction and loop around when the coast was clear. Easing each booted foot along as quietly as she could, she kept her eyes on the ground, scanning for twigs that might snap and give her away, or rocks that might result in a noisy fall. She'd made it several yards when a rough palm clamped over her mouth, holding in her scream.

TWELVE

Ethan felt Kendra tense under his palm.

"It's me," he whispered, but not before she drove an elbow into his stomach. He lurched back, doubled over, and Titus shoved a wet nose in his face. "I'm okay," he assured the dog.

Kendra whirled, hands on hips, glaring at him. "What were you thinking?" she whispered in a tone just south of furious.

"I was thinking," he muttered back, "that you might cry out and give away our location."

She was breathing hard. "You scared me."

He managed an upright posture and a half-hearted breath. "I'm sorry." Titus stood on hind legs and licked Ethan's face, double-checking his handler. "Okay, down, you big galoot." He pressed a hand to his throbbing gut. "I saw the sentry. He's twenty yards to the north."

"I saw him, too," she said. "I was busy avoiding him when you decided to scare the wits out of me with your ninja skills."

"Seems like you still have your wits to me," he said. "I think you might have damaged my spleen."

"Serves you right for that bonehead move." She shook

her head, disgusted, then her expression shifted into concern. "Did I really hurt you?"

He smiled. "No, ma'am. I was just looking for some sympathy."

She exhaled. "Okay. Sorry about the elbow." She offered a small pat to his shoulder. "If your spleen is fully functional, we'd better move."

"Yes, ma'am." They continued looping around away from the river, making their mucky way over the forest detritus.

"Did you recognize the soldier?" Kendra asked.

"Tall, dark and deadly, that's all I got."

"Me, too. Probably a marine."

"Probably." He picked up the pace. In spite of the doggy raincoat Ethan had put on him, Titus kept stopping to shake the moisture from his ears. "He's more used to dry conditions than rain."

"Me, too," she said. They continued on, the irregular slope requiring all their mental and physical energies. The night ticked away and fatigue began to prey on Ethan, but Kendra did not complain nor slow, so they pushed on, Titus as tireless as ever.

After an arduous uphill climb, Ethan signaled a stop. They'd arrived at a mad jumble of rocks, some piled as high as fifty feet. "Good lookout point." He ordered Titus to sit at Kendra's side under the shelter of a rock overhang. He began to climb, the footholds easy to find but slippery. When he reached a smooth section of stone, he lay down and peered through his night-vision binocs. He located one soldier easily enough, probably a newbie to the SERE training or cold enough to risk a fire where he thought he wouldn't be seen. He'd be captured quickly. Nothing else moved that he could detect. To the east lay

the road they would take to Baylor before sunup in order
to reach the base by the appointed hour.

His watch read 2:00 a.m., still three hours to evade
capture. At that point, the evasion portion would be complete and all they would have to do was get back to base.
Best to hole up. He figured this was the optimal location and time to do it. Good view, plenty of hiding spots,
shelter from the rain.

He returned to ground level and found Kendra and
Titus gone. His stomach dropped to his boots. For a moment he second-guessed himself, but it was precisely the
spot he'd left them with strict orders not to leave.

Frantically he examined the ground for any signs of
attack. Why hadn't Titus barked? He plunged into the
shrubs, wildly scanning, calling as loud as he dared. A
gleam of movement, a subtle shifting in the darkness
burned into his vision. He drew his weapon, figuring
blanks were better than nothing as he raced forward,
keeping low under an overgrown thicket with razor-sharp
thorns. He must have misjudged their safety, missed a
sentry or missed Sullivan. Nerves kicked up all over his
body.

Titus darted out from behind a bush, running at Ethan,
blood showing on his mouth. Ethan's breath crystallized
in his lungs. Where was Kendra? The dog bounded up,
and Ethan inhaled the smell of berries.

Not blood. Juice.

"You rotten dog…"

"Quiet," Kendra said, stepping out of the shrubs.
"You're making enough noise to bring in the marines
for sure."

"Where…where did you go?" he sputtered.

"I got us some dinner."

He couldn't believe his ears. "What?" he finally managed.

She held out a handkerchief full of glistening black-berries. "There's a whole thicket of them."

He goggled, fear crystallizing into anger. "You shouldn't have moved. I thought something happened to you."

She raised an eyebrow. "Did I scare you?"

If the light had been better, he figured he'd have seen a glint of satisfaction on her face. "Dumb move."

"I weighed the risks."

"You didn't have the right to take my dog off his assignment."

"He shouldn't have let me, right?"

Ethan glowered at Titus. "Right, and we're going to have to do some retraining."

The dog snaked a tongue over his lips. Kendra laughed. "He doesn't look the least bit sorry."

"Well, you should be," he snapped. "This isn't a game, Kendra."

She went still. "It's never been a game for me, Ethan."

"Then stop treating it like one. One bullet and you're dead, don't you understand that?" One bullet, like Martelli, like the others. One shot you didn't see coming, from an enemy you'd let stray from your mind for one second.

Even in the darkness he could see her eyes glimmer. "I know what it's like to be hunted."

Hunted. The word disintegrated his anger. Hunted, by a man she thought she'd loved. Stung, shot at, terrorized. She'd lived her own kind of war for longer than he had. *Yeah, dumb comment, Webb.*

"Let's get to shelter," he said before anything else came out of his mouth.

Titus trotted to his side. "I mean it, dog. You need retraining," he said. "Since when do you take orders from her?"

Ethan scouted the area until he located the crevice he'd spotted earlier, a depression punched into the rock wall. It was not high enough for them to stand up, but it was comfortable for two sitting adults and a sprawling dog. The floor was mostly dry and clean after he kicked the debris away. By the time they entered, Kendra was shivering, her teeth chattering together.

"Sorry, we can't risk a fire."

"It's okay. At least we have dinner." She laid the berries out between them. Perfectly ripe, thumb-sized, succulent.

He ate a handful. "Best berries I've ever had," he declared, "but it still doesn't make it okay what you did wandering off."

"So Titus and I are still in the doghouse?"

"He's definitely in the doghouse." He rubbed his sticky hands clean on his wet pant leg. "But, uh, what I said back there, that wasn't cool."

She wiped her fingers on her pants. "It's okay. In a way there's some truth to it. I think Andy thought of our relationship as a game. How far could he string me along, how much could he push." She leaned against the rock, her gaze drifting to the rain falling outside the cave. "He was raised by a single parent, too, an alcoholic." Her smile was rueful. "We had a lot in common."

"Not the right stuff, though."

She shrugged. "I didn't think I was worth too much when I met him and he agreed. Just strung me along, like I said, and I was dumb enough to let him."

"What was the turning point?"

She didn't answer for a moment, and then she rolled up her right sleeve to show a long narrow scar. "I found a stray cat starving under our apartment step. I took her in and Andy grumbled, but he didn't resist too much until she used his guitar case as a scratching post."

He saw the play of emotion as the memory unfolded itself.

"He went after her with a kitchen knife. I fended him off with a chair, but he cut me." Her fingers stroked the edge of her sleeve, as if she was comforting the terrified cat. "The cat was able to hide, though."

"Baby?" he said.

She nodded. "I realized that we weren't alike, Andy and me, not fundamentally, not deep down, but I wasn't sure how to get out of the mess I'd made. A few days later he told me we were going to rob a mini mart and if I didn't go along with the plan, he would kill me and the cat. That's when I decided to call Jillian." She looked at him then, tears glistening in her eyes. "See why Baby means so much to me?"

He took her hand and pulled her into the circle of his arm. "Yeah, I sure do."

She snuggled next to him, leaning against his chest as if they'd known each other forever. The scent of the woods clung to her wet hair, as alluring as the silk of her cheek brushing his chin. He kissed her temple, pressed her close as if he could blast away her terrible past.

Not possible.

And not the right thing anyway. Her past was what made her who she was, turned her to God. The fact that she'd shared it with him, her worst moment, made something inside him crack open. He wanted to kiss her as she turned her face to his. She was so beautiful, like an angel painted on the wall of stone behind her. He cupped her face, bent close and fitted her mouth to his. A current of electricity jolted through him, the completion of a circuit he hadn't known about. She kissed him back, warm, giving, tender.

Nothing ever felt quite like this. Comfort, belonging, wholeness, peace.

But something wriggled in his memory. He flashed back to Jillian, how he'd bared his soul to her, how she'd stripped him of his dignity and his pride. Pain and humiliation and shame all roared back in a split second.

Not again, not ever.

He eased Kendra to his side and they leaned against the cold rock, breathing unsteadily.

"I, uh, sorry," he mumbled. "Got caught up. Won't happen again."

He thought he heard her sigh. From disappointment? Or relief?

"It's okay," she whispered and he couldn't decipher the emotion in it.

Get her through it and don't let yourself want anything more. Wanting led to yearning, to trusting, to a heart flayed wide-open. His mind remained stone-cold logical, but his heart hungered in a way that scared him silly.

Cold seeped inside him, wrestling with a warmth that she kindled in the dark places. In agonizing slow motion, the minutes crept by.

It felt like morning would never come.

The hours wore on and they took turns keeping watch. While Ethan hunkered down somewhere outside with his binoculars in hand, she lay on the ground with Titus snuggled against her back. The unaccustomed freedom that she had finally shared her burden with Ethan gave way to grief.

Got caught up. Won't happen again.

His words were a harsh reminder. Ethan wasn't interested. He'd said so from the beginning. Her feelings had changed, his had not. *Wake up and smell the coffee, Kendra.* Besides, why would she have wanted more kisses in the middle of SERE training with threats coming at them from all sides? Was she losing her mind?

It was her turn to take over the watch, so she sat up. Though it was still dark, she figured it had to be sometime near the end of the evasion portion of the drill. Sullivan wasn't going to make a move, or so it seemed, but at least they'd survived the SERE refresher, satisfied Masters's whim and could move on with their investigation.

She heaved herself up, muscles complaining, back aching from her time on the hard ground. Rejoicing to see that the rain had stopped, she stepped out, and that's when horror fired her nerves into flame.

Ethan lay stomach down on the ground, a soldier standing over him with a gun aimed at his skull.

"Time to die," the soldier said.

Kendra didn't hesitate, she swung her rifle like a club, smashing the soldier in the back of the knees. He went down like a felled tree. Titus was out of the cave in a flash of fur, diving on the man and nearly ripping off his uniform.

Ethan leaped to his feet.

"Get him off, Ethan," the marine hollered, rolling into a ball to protect his face.

Ethan hollered at Titus, who promptly returned to Ethan's side and sat, staring down his enemy.

The soldier sat up and Kendra thought he looked vaguely familiar.

"Hector," Ethan said with a smile. "Fancy meeting you here. Out for a stroll?"

Hector was the marine who'd investigated when she'd

been shot at. He was not smiling. He got to his feet. "Not cool to bring your dog along to save your bacon."

"He didn't save me," Ethan said. "She did."

Kendra wriggled her fingers. "Hey, Hector. Sorry about that."

He eyed her name patch. "Thought your name was Kendra. How come you're Jillian Masters all of a sudden?"

Ethan shook his head. "Long story, but for now, she's Jillian. You can confirm that with Colonel Masters."

"Jillian, as in your ex-wife Jillian?"

He nodded.

"Man," Hector said, "you airmen sure know how to get yourself into a pile of trouble, don't you?"

"That's an affirmative," Ethan said.

"Well, anyway, you're dead 'cuz I got you down on the ground before ole slugger and Fido here saved you."

"No, sir," Ethan said, holding his ancient Timex. "It's zero five ten hours, Marine. You're ten minutes past the deadline. We won."

Hector laughed. "All right. Leave it to Webb to land on his feet." His smile vanished. "Lieutenant Masters, I am charged with delivering a message to you."

Kendra stiffened.

"Yes?" she said.

Hector brushed off his uniform, jammed a hand into his pack and pulled out a piece of paper. He held it out to Kendra, who took it. "Safe travels back to base."

Ethan waved and Hector began to clamber down the rocky trail.

Kendra opened the note.

I need to speak with you both immediately. Urgent.
—Officer Alonso Carpenter.

THIRTEEN

Kendra puzzled over the message as they hiked back to the road. She desperately wished her cell phone signal would kick in.

"We'll be back in less than an hour. We can call from base or when our cell phones are operation. Whichever comes first," Ethan said.

In spite of the adrenaline, Kendra found her legs were leaden as she tried her best to keep up with Ethan and Titus. Muscles screamed for attention, made worse by the cold infiltrating her limbs via her damp clothing. After stopping twice to remove stickers from Titus's paws, they finally made it to the frontage road that would take them to base. A smooth surface. She felt like cheering.

Behind them, barely discernible in the gloom, were two other soldiers dragging themselves back to base, tired, hungry, no doubt as relieved as she was that it was all over. Somewhere sprinkled along the road were the rest of the trainees.

She scratched at a row of mosquito bites on her neck, a new series of welts to replace the wasp stings that had died away. What had the whole exercise gained them? Not much. Sullivan had not showed his hand. Heidi Jenks had proved just as much of an enigma. Kendra had bared her soul to Ethan in the cave, only to have him back away. Now every muscle was screaming for her to stop, but they had a generous three miles to go back to base. She had a whole new admiration for the men and women of the US military.

A hot shower, she told herself. She'd have a hot shower and a cheeseburger and then call Officer Carpenter. That mantra echoed in her mind as she forced one soggy boot in front of the other. The trail funneled toward a ten-foot bridge that spanned a narrow section of river. Below, the water roared, swollen from the spring rains. Still wet and clammy, she'd had quite enough water for one day.

She'd moved a couple of feet onto the bridge, Ethan a few feet ahead of her, when a shout cut through the gray morning.

She stopped, whirled and then she heard it.

One shot, followed by three more.

A soldier raced up the road, awkward in his heavy pack and muddy boots. "Incoming," he hollered. "Guy's driving crazy. I tried to fire some warning shots."

"What?" Kendra yelled.

Tires squealed and a car with no lights careened past the soldier, who futilely fired another blank round at the tires.

Kendra froze, staring as the car hurtled toward her.

"Run," Ethan shouted. He was beside her now, Titus barking wildly. "Get across the bridge to the woods on the other side." He took up a position dead center in the road and began firing blank rounds at the car.

"Ethan, no," she yelled. "They'll run you down."

"Go," he snarled. "Now."

She ran farther onto the bridge, tossing aside her heavy pack. The car edged closer. Had Ethan got out of the way?

Her boots weighed her feet down, but she ran as fast as

she could, her pulse thundering, lungs straining, gasping for breath. Now the car was so close it kicked up gravel that struck the back of her neck. She turned to look, horrified to see the bumper inches away, the shadow of a figure in the driver's seat cloaked in darkness, its gloved fingers gripping the wheel. She couldn't see the driver's face but he emitted the same kind of crazy she'd seen in Andy.

Crazy, mixed with hatred and a need for vengeance that would only be satisfied with her death.

With every ounce of energy she could muster, she sprinted for the other side, for the safety of the trees, but the end of the bridge might as well have been miles away.

Despair hit hard and heavy as she realized she was not going to make it. She would be crushed under the wheels, the life expunged from her in a violent punch of metal on bone.

No. God, give me strength. Just a little more.

But she did not have the stamina to escape the car. There was only one way to survive…if she had the courage.

In one explosive leap, she vaulted onto the bridge railing, sprawling across the rail, folded in half by the force. Time slowed down as she teetered there. The car scraped the side of the bridge, sending sparks, tremors that shook her body as she heaved herself over and plummeted down into the water.

Ethan scrambled up from the spot where he'd dived with Titus as the car roared past him. "Kendra!" His shout was lost in the grind of metal on metal as the vehicle scraped the rail, crossed the bridge and disappeared.

His heart hammering and his stomach knotted, he ran.

He pounded onto the bridge, scanning, searching, dreading what he would find.

Where was Kendra?

He found the impact site where the car had skimmed the side of the bridge. No Kendra. Titus put his paws up over the railing and barked. Ethan threw himself against the rail, staring down into the oil-black eddies.

"Kendra!" he shouted as loud as he could. Forget the investigation, forget her cover. His heart burned, his soul ached with one thought only.

He had to find her.

Reversing course, he met the other soldier and Hector tearing up the road.

"Sit rep, Airman," Hector barked.

"Vehicle headed north on Pine Hill Road," Ethan told him. "Front and rear plates obscured. She...Jillian Masters is in the water. We need a rescue crew."

Hector pulled a radio from his belt and relayed the information. "Water's moving fast," he said to Ethan.

He understood. By the time the rescue crew was in place, she might very well be dead. He got the flashlight from his pack and called Titus.

Hector reached out a hand to stop him. "Ethan—"

"I'm going to find her. You and the police get the car."

Several soldiers had gathered around.

"That driver was nuts," one said. "Like he was gunning right for her."

"How'd they pick her out?" his partner said. "We all look like filthy, dirty grunts."

Ethan's gut clenched. The driver knew Kendra was with Ethan and the dog. Titus had been a neon sign. *Come and get her.*

"Sir, permission to aid in the search for the victim," one of the soldiers said.

Hector considered. "You up to it, Soldier?"

"Sir, yes, sir."

His compatriot chimed in as well. "Me, too, sir."

Hector nodded. "Report in every fifteen."

"Yes, sir," the men said.

Ethan felt a swell of gratitude for his brothers in arms. They shoved flashlights in their pockets and Hector handed one a first-aid kit along with a coil of rope and a radio.

"We'll take the north bank, Lieutenant," one of the soldiers said.

"I've got the south," Ethan confirmed.

"Good hunting, Marines." Hector said. "You, too, Airman."

Ethan and Titus raced in the direction the current must have taken her. He prayed the water under the bridge was deep enough to absorb her fall without causing broken arms and legs or worse. The roar was intense along the shore. He and Titus pushed through the tall grasses. He was not sure Titus was a good enough tracker to detect Kendra's scent in the water and the specialty they'd been training for recently wasn't finding the living. Nonetheless, Titus stuck his nose to every muck-filled pocket and rock, wriggling his way along. *Trust your dog.*

Under the dense shadows of the trees, Ethan shone the flashlight and shouted her name with every few feet. He heard the echo of the soldiers on the far bank doing the same. He shouted again and stopped to listen. No answer but the roar of water.

His flashlight picked out a massive tree trunk, flipped on its side in the water, a mad tangle of roots protruding in every direction. The beam danced over the wet wood, and he was about to pass by when the light caught a flick of white in the darkness. He splashed in up to his knees, fighting the current, rubbing his eyes to be sure. This time he knew he was not mistaken. Curled around an exposed root was a tightly clenched fist.

Kendra was dizzy from her tumultuous journey, numb both from the icy water and her vicious impact into the river. She'd swallowed a lot of water and the cold was beginning to ice over her limbs, loosen her precarious grip on the root or branch or whatever it was that she had tumbled into. She had to hold on, recover enough to make it to shore, or call for help in case Ethan was within earshot.

She remembered his defiant stance as he faced the car head on, firing shots into the front windshield. What if…?

Stop thinking and start moving, she ordered herself, but her fingers were frozen into a desperate claw and she found she was shivering too much to even fill her lungs with air to call out.

Cold.

It was all she could think of.

So cold.

When something landed in the water near her she was too chilled to look.

"I've got you," a voice said.

Ethan. Where had he come from? She wanted to fall into his arms but she could not move, could not let go. Her body would simply not obey.

Titus grabbed hold of her uniform sleeve and began to tug.

"Stop," she whispered. "I'll drown."

Ethan's face swam into view through the spray. "Let go, honey. I've got you now."

Can't. Cold. Scared.

He put his face closer and kissed her. His lips were

soft on hers, and she wanted to disappear inside the tenderness, the comfort, the warmth. The kiss was all she could feel. It was everything.

"It's okay," he said, his eyes riveted to hers. "Trust me. I'm going to get you out of here."

Out of here. Trust me.

He pried gently at her grip. "Put your hands around my neck. Here. Like this." He prized her fingers from the wet wood and she almost screamed, but he placed them around his shoulders. She clung to him, his body strong and steady against the current.

Trust me.

She pressed her face to his, her lips against his stubbled jaw as he yelled to someone on shore. A rope splashed down in the water and Ethan fastened it around them. After a tug, a lurch that made her want to cry out again, they were in the thick of the current, being pummeled by the raging water.

Sensing her rising panic, he pressed her head to his neck. "It's okay. You're okay. They're pulling us out."

Ethan called to Titus, and when the dog did not follow quickly enough, he grabbed him with the arm that wasn't fastened around her. Inch by inch, they were loosened from the iron grip of the water until she heard the mud squishing under Ethan's boots.

The others, soldiers, too, she realized, took her arms and moved her away from the water onto a flat rock outcropping. She felt rather than heard the man next to her snap to attention. "He's gone back in."

She jackknifed to a sitting position.

"Ethan? Why?" She thought she screamed the words but only a whisper came out.

The soldier raced back to the water's edge, running alongside the riverbed, shouting something she could not hear. She tried to crawl, but the other soldier held her back.

"Stay here, ma'am. They'll handle it."

"Handle it?" she gasped. "The water is a roller coaster and he's wearing boots and gear. You have to help him. He'll drown. Why would he go back in? Why?"

"The dog, ma'am."

"Titus?"

"He couldn't make it out. Got loose and the water sucked him back in. The lieutenant went after him."

She stared. He'd risked his life for her and now he was doing the same thing for a dog. Not just a dog, a fellow soldier, a brother.

"I want to help," she said, trying to get her wobbling legs to cooperate as he unfolded a metallic blanket and draped it over her. She pushed it away.

"Ma'am, stay here. You're nearing hypothermic."

"I'll warm up."

"No, ma'am." He unclipped the radio from his belt. "Medic will be here shortly."

"I have to help Ethan. Titus…" She pictured the big goofy dog, stained with blackberry juice, trying to persuade Ethan that it was bedtime. Ethan's best friend.

She made it to her knees when the radio squawked.

"Is he… Did they find him?"

A funny look came over his face and he pointed up-river. She sank back to the ground, fear thick as the night air.

Ethan clomped over the rocks, the other soldier at his side, Titus draped over his shoulders, a still, dark shadow. Her heart twisted into a knot until Titus raised his head and barked, a throaty, beautiful, raucous sound.

She blinked back tears.

Ethan knelt and eased Titus to the ground.

"Nutty dog thinks he's an Olympic swimmer. I told you to get out of the water. Didn't you hear me?" He pressed his nose to the dog's wet head. Titus slurped a lick over Ethan's forehead. Ethan ordered him to a sit next to Kendra. She reached out a tentative arm. Ethan did not correct the dog, so he snuggled up next to her, shivering. She wrapped the silver blanket around them both, cuddling as much as she could of the wet animal.

Ethan crouched next to her. "How are you?" he asked gently.

"I'm f-f-fine," she said, teeth chattering.

He pulled the blanket around her tighter. "It's okay not to be."

No, it's not, she thought. *You could have died. Titus could have died, all to help me.* It was not tolerable even to think it.

The medics arrived carrying a stretcher between them since there was no way to get a vehicle close enough. They checked her vitals after Ethan coaxed Titus away and bundled him in his own blanket.

"I'm not going to the base clinic," Kendra said. "I'm going home."

The medic arched an eyebrow. "Ma'am, you need to be checked out by a doctor."

"No, I don't." *I need to get home, lock the doors and take the hottest shower I can manage.*

The medic looked at Ethan. "Lieutenant?"

Ethan nodded and came to her side. "Jillian," he said, "I'm not gonna argue with you about this."

"Good."

"And I know I'm in for it later."

"What—" Before she could say another word, he scooped her up and laid her on the stretcher. If her body wasn't trembling like a leaf in the storm, she would have leaped off immediately and given him a sock in the shoulder. As it was, all she could do was lie there and glare at him as the medics strapped her to a board and hoisted her between them like a sack of laundry.

"Ethan," she snapped.

"I know, you're gonna make me pay. I get it." He turned to the medics. "I'll follow you."

They nodded and carried her away, helpless, miserable and furious.

FOURTEEN

Ethan refused to debrief one word of the incident with Hector and his security team until they summoned a local veterinarian to come and check Titus over. Unsettled and on edge, Titus wasn't having any of it until Ethan forced the growling dog to cooperate. Still, the veterinarian was a shade paler by the time he completed his work. Ethan didn't blame him. With a bite strength of more than two hundred pounds of pressure, Titus wasn't to be trifled with and he hadn't even gotten his man. Ethan felt like growling, too.

The vet wiped his brow. "I gave him some antibiotics just in case he swallowed something nasty, and treated the abrasion on his paw. He's earned a cheeseburger or something for not eating me."

"Aww, he wouldn't have eaten you," Ethan said with a smile, "not unless I told him to. Might have taken a little bite, just to taste."

"Good to know," said the vet as he left.

The doctor was still with Kendra when Ethan settled in the waiting room where Hector stood leaning against the wall. He'd been more than patient…for a marine. Titus sprawled out on a sofa and promptly started snoring.

"I looped Officer Carpenter in," Hector said. "He's on his way."

"Even though you didn't want to?"

He lifted a shoulder. "Just like last time, the incident wasn't on base property so it's out of my hands, which irritates me." Hector drilled him with a look. "Ethan, what's the real story here?"

"What do you mean?"

"Someone's trying real hard to kill Jillian Masters. First the gunshots, now the car. We've been briefed on your Red Rose Killer, at least what the air force has been willing to share. Is this who we're dealing with here?"

"I don't know."

Hector's dark eyes shifted. "Can I tell you what I think, bro?"

"I would like to hear it."

"I think this isn't the work of Boyd Sullivan."

Ethan blew out a breath. "Okay. How'd you get there?"

"Because when he wanted to kill here at Baylor and at Canyon, he did. Our marine was shot through the head, up close and personal. Your trainers were, too."

"We figured that also, but it could be he's had to get more creative now, since both the US Air Force and the Marines are after him."

"Could be." Hector clicked his pen.

Again, Ethan waited. *Click, click.*

He would only get what Hector was willing to share with him and that would have to be enough, since Ethan was not at liberty to tell his friend the whole story.

After two more clicks, Hector started talking. "I heard one of the guys he killed over at Canyon was your buddy," he said slowly. "You two close?"

Ethan gazed at his boots. "Yeah. Landon was a quality person. Gentle with the dogs and respectful to everyone, you know?"

Hector nodded.

Ethan let his mind wander back to the past. "He was going to propose to his girl and he was driving us all crazy trying to figure out the perfect romantic gesture. He was planning to wait until winter and build a snowman holding the box with the ring." Hector laughed. "I told him he was crazy and we teased him that she'd dump him way before the snow fell." Ethan shook his head. "Didn't dampen his spirit one bit. Asked me to be his best man."

Best man, who wasn't even there when he was killed in cold blood. "He was an excellent soldier and a good man."

"Yeah, our marine was a good guy, too. Married, with a baby on the way." More pen clicks. "How's his wife gonna explain Daddy's murder to the kid someday?"

Ethan felt the bile rose in his throat. "I'm sorry."

"Me, too." Hector gave it another moment of thought. "Okay. We're going after Sullivan with both barrels then, but you better keep your eyes peeled for a different enemy, 'cuz like I said, I got another reason to believe this ain't him."

"What's that?"

"One of my marines got a funny impression."

Ethan's instincts prickled. "Funny how?"

"That the driver of the car was a female."

Ethan stared at Hector.

"Just an impression, mind you, nothing concrete. Something about the face… A glimpse really. I had to badger him into telling me since he wasn't certain."

Hector's radio chattered. "Gotta go make a phone call."

"Thanks, Hector."

"Watch your back, man, and you'd better watch hers, too."

The doctor appeared at the door and crooked a finger at Ethan. Titus awakened and followed him into a nearby room. Kendra was sitting up on the exam table, a hospital gown pulled around her. Though her face was pale under the freckles and her hair curling in dirty spirals, her look was determined. She was telegraphing him a message.

Heads up.

"Jillian tells me you two are going to get remarried." He swallowed. "Yes, sir."

"Not to be rude, but I've heard talk that your breakup was rather...nasty."

"We're putting all that behind us, Doc." He went for a polite smile. "What's her prognosis?"

"Bumps, bruises and a mysterious condition which I can't explain."

His heart thumped. "What?"

"We're a big base here at Baylor, so I've never treated Lieutenant Masters before personally, but we're pretty good at keeping records. Know what my records show, Airman?"

"What's that, sir?"

"That Jillian Masters is five foot eleven."

"Is that right?"

"Yes, it is, and I can't help noticing that this woman is not that tall. In addition, the blood types don't match. Shall I go on?"

"No, sir," Ethan said.

Kendra sucked in a breath. "There is a good explanation, Doctor."

"Great." He picked up the phone. "You'll be able to explain that to the cops when they arrive."

There was a rap on the door frame and Alonso Carpenter stuck his head in.

"No need to call, Doctor," he said. "I'm already here."

Kendra wasn't sure how to feel at Carpenter's arrival. Relieved? Frightened? At the moment she was fighting the numbness that crept into her when she'd hurtled over the rail into the river. She knew for certain whatever Carpenter had to say was going to be big and she did not want to be sitting wrapped in a clinic gown while he said it.

"I'd like to change, please," she announced.

All three men stared at her as if she'd just spoken in Latin. She gestured to the Marine sweat suit on the chair. "They loaned me clothes. I'd like to change before this discussion goes any further."

"All right," the doctor said. "We'll wait in my office next door."

The men and the dog shuffled out and Kendra stripped quickly, pulling on the heavyweight sweats, her muscles complaining as she did so. The dry cloth felt luxurious on her skin but it did not quell the ire beginning to kindle in her belly.

"Didn't I tell Ethan not to bring me here?" she muttered. How exactly was she supposed to explain things to the doctor? There was no way but to reveal the truth and hope he was discreet enough to keep the secret and in no way connected to Boyd Sullivan. Then she'd have to explain to Colonel Masters how her cover had been blown.

Her skin crawled as she pulled on her wet boots, but there was no help for it. She wasn't about to confront the doctor and Carpenter in bare feet.

She snagged a rubber band from one of the neat jars on the doctor's cabinet and twisted her filthy hair into a ponytail. Not good, but at least she didn't look like a be-draggled child just pulled out of the kiddie pool.

She tried to force her brain back into investigator mode. The person who had run her down was familiar with the area and knew what road the soldiers would be taking back to base when the drill was completed. Someone local? Or someone who had asked questions, ferreted out the information? Someone like Heidi Jenks? Or Andy?

Her brain addled, but shoulders straight, she ignored the squeaking of her boots and made her way with as much dignity as she could muster into the adjoining office.

The doctor was gone.

"He got a call from Colonel Masters," Ethan said.

Kendra sighed. "Well, that's a relief. Masters is gifted in twisting the truth to suit his needs."

"So's his daughter." He looked as though he wished he hadn't said it. She examined him further and realized he appeared as though he'd been through a combat zone. His face was scratched, one eye swollen, his uniform still muddy and damp. Guilt licked her insides and her anger that he'd delivered her onto the stretcher melted away.

He's been through this because of you, Kendra, not because of Masters. For her it was a job. For him...duty to his ex-wife? That Southern gentlemen complex? An order? And why did his bruised mouth look so inviting at that moment when she knew full well he regretted their earlier kiss? She hugged herself to cage in the feelings. "I don't suppose there was any success finding the driver."

"No." Carpenter patted his pockets for the pen that was shoved behind his ear.

She pointed.

He smiled. "Thanks. Marines say the plates were

concealed. Someone was being careful. They lost the tracks when the dirt road rejoined the highway. My cops couldn't do any better."

Ethan blew out a breath. "There was a wrinkle here," he told her. "One of the soldiers said he thought the driver was female."

Kendra's mouth dropped open. "You're kidding."

"No. Not a total surprise, I guess." Ethan eyed Carpenter. "We figured Sullivan has a female accomplice, if this is even Sullivan's work to begin with." He scrubbed a hand over his forehead. "I'm not sure anymore."

Ethan was obviously exhausted. It had taken every ounce of his energy to wrestle her from the river and then do the same for Titus. Even the dog seemed tired, sprawled on the tile floor. There was nothing more to be gained until they both got some sleep.

"We need to get some rest," she said. She turned to Carpenter as she remembered. "You left a message for me. You said it was urgent."

"Yes. I thought you should know that Andy Bleakman did not check in with his parole officer two days ago."

Fear punched her in the gut.

"And the thing is," Carpenter said, "I'm not sure he really did last week, either."

"What do you mean?" Ethan demanded. "We were told he checked in. If not, he should have been tracked down and arrested immediately."

"Should have been, yes. There's been some confusion in the parole department. Overworked, underpaid and..."

"And?" She stared hard at the cop.

"And possible corruption."

"Oh, that's perfect." She groaned. "He paid off his parole officer, didn't he?"

Carpenter nodded. "It appears that way. The officer

in question has been suspended pending an investigation, which means—"

"That Andy's been free since the moment he stepped out of prison," Kendra said with only a small tremor in her voice.

Free.

Mindy's words about the stranger who called her house echoed in her mind. *Looking forward to seeing you soon.* Andy had tracked Jillian down because he figured she'd be staying with her, the faithful friend who'd helped double-cross him.

Free to come and kill me.

FIFTEEN

Ethan didn't like the silence. Kendra sat in the passenger seat of his truck, nonreactive, even when Titus rolled a tongue down the back of her neck. He'd gotten her to drink some water, but she'd refused any of the snacks he'd kept in the car. Titus was not so picky, wolfing down a handful of dog treats before they'd started for home.

"Later we'll interview the women Sullivan had contact with besides the ones we've already investigated in depth, in case the marine was right and it was a woman who tried to run you down. One's on base at Canyon, an ammo specialist, the other's just outside Canyon and Linc will talk to her."

She offered no answer, except for a faint nod. They passed Mindy's house, quiet and still. He could tell by the crimp of her mouth and the laced fingers that she longed to go collect Baby, but Kendra was not herself.

"And Heidi Jenks," he continued. "I'll find out what Linc got from her. He's already going over the prison visitor list again, to see if we missed something."

Kendra sighed. "Ethan, you and I both know this isn't Sullivan."

"No, we don't. That's an assumption, one we can't afford to make."

She shook her head as he pulled the truck into the driveway of Jillian's house. "It's Andy. I can feel it." She sniffed, pulling the sleeve of her borrowed sweatshirt across her teary eyes.

"Hey," he said, catching her hand. "We'll get him. We'll get them both."

There was another long pause, and she removed her hand from his. "Ethan, we can't do this together. I want you to stay away from me."

He cocked his head. "Are you dumping me as a partner? It's the dog, isn't it? He's so bad for my mojo."

She didn't even crack a smile. "I'm going to continue the Sullivan investigation, but I'm Andy's target and if you're near me, you're his target, too. That's not what you were ordered to do."

"News flash, but I don't always follow orders and I'm not afraid of Andy. As a matter of fact, I hope he is coming, because we're going to have ourselves a set before I arrest him."

"It's not your battle."

"Yes, it is."

"I don't need you."

"Yes, you do."

First he saw a spark of anger in her eyes, then a flush of vulnerability. Then she asked the question that brought his own vulnerability front and center.

"Why? Why would you put your life at risk for mine?"

He tried for flippant. "Dog handlers' motto. We find what you fear. You fear Andy, so I'm gonna find him and sort him out. Simple as that."

"Duty?" There was a current of emotion in her eyes, running deep and swift as the river. Her lips parted, gleaming soft in the darkness. "That's the only reason?"

He didn't want to, his mind screamed against it, but he

reached out, trailing fingers over the satin of her cheek, her chin. And then he was moving toward her, his mouth seeking hers. For a moment, she was reaching out, too, her hands pulling him closer, until he stopped himself. He pressed his forehead against hers and tried for a steady breath. He held her there, forcing himself with every ounce of self-control to forgo kissing his ex-wife's double.

What is wrong with you, Webb?

The trauma of the last twenty-four hours had pressed his emotions into overdrive, overriding all common sense and logic. There would be no more determined women in his life, no more access to his already wrecked heart. No more Jillians.

He felt her move away and he did the same. Clearing his throat, he sought the safety of the driver's side. Though they still tingled from the feel of her, he put his hands on the wheel. "Kendra, I…"

But she was already out of the car and striding toward the house. He remembered his brother's favorite saying.

Smooth as sandpaper, Ethan.

He looked at Titus. "I didn't handle that right, did I?"

Titus gave him a weary expression that probably meant, "So what's new?"

Heaving himself from the car, he waited until Kendra was safely inside before he went to seek the solace of a hot shower, a heartfelt prayer to thank God for their survival.

Though his body hollered for a couple hours of sleep, Ethan's stomach willed him into the kitchen in midmorning. He left Titus snoring in a pile of blankets and went into the main house. The dog had earned some extra downtime.

Rounding up eggs, cheese and mushrooms, Ethan

started an omelet in one pan and a mess of bacon in the
other. Since he could not love her or any other woman
with his present state of brokenness, he would jolly well
fix her problems, the first one being her unsated appe-
tite. The aroma of bacon and eggs had the desired effect,
Kendra appeared in a fresh Marine battle dress uniform,
her hair neatly caught up low on her neck. He'd hoped
she would not bring up their near kiss and she didn't,
though he thought he saw a faint pink blush underneath
the bruise on her cheek when she encountered him.

"Feel okay?"

"Hungry," she said.

"I can fix that."

She poured herself a cup of coffee from the machine,
sighing as she sipped the brew. "Did you talk to your
people at Canyon?"

"Yeah. I have the interview scheduled. You game to
come with?" He feared she would say no, and wondered
what kind of plan he'd need to come up with if she did.
There was no way he was leaving her alone, whether she
liked it or not.

She ate a mouthful of eggs. "I'm in. I worked this
morning on tracking Andy's movements, but I didn't
get very far. He's not using his old credit cards, nor the
same car."

"We'll get him." He sat across from her. The click of
utensils and the sipping of coffee wasn't enough to break
up the silence. He wished he could undo his bonehead
behavior in the cave and then the truck, close the un-
professional gap he'd created between them. He had the
uneasy feeling he'd led her on somehow, made her care
about him in a way that just wouldn't do.

"Kendra, I'm sorry about—"

"Nothing to apologize for," she said quickly. "You

saved my life. I don't want you to be in danger again, but I can see that you're not going to budge until Sullivan is caught."

"And Andy is in prison."

"That's not your problem."

"But like you said, I'm not going to budge."

She held up a hand. "Ethan, I'm too tired to go through this at the moment. For now, we'll follow the trail we have on Sullivan and see where it goes."

And I'll work my own leads to find Andy. He'd already put in calls while Kendra showered to the contacts Hector had given him, locals in town who would recognize Andy from the mug shot he'd gotten from Carpenter, and emailed them. The coffee shop owner, the gas station attendant, a couple of bartenders.

"Fair enough," he said. They finished their breakfast on somewhat neutral ground. "Let's go get your cat before I wake up the beast."

"Some beast," Kendra said with a snort. "I can practically hear him snoring from here."

He was so glad to see her smile, he grinned back like a fool. "He worked overtime."

"You're right," she said. "He went into the river right along with you to save my life, so I owe him a steak dinner." She eyed him. "And you, too."

"Ooooh, dangerous offer," he said. "Titus and I can eat our body weight in beef."

She laughed, even better than the smile. "I'll start saving my pennies."

They washed the dishes together, shoulder to shoulder, and things were easy again between them. Once the kitchen was clean and bottles of water and kibble packed into the truck, at 10:00, she tapped on Mindy's door.

Mindy pulled it open, wearing a pink robe, curlers

bristling all over her head. Baby snuggled in her arms, mewing when she saw Kendra. Kendra took the bony cat, murmuring baby talk against her small head.

"Thank you for taking care of her." She smoothed the cat's fur.

"Oh, she wasn't much trouble," Mindy said. "We watched silly television and ate ice cream until we fell asleep. Well, I ate the ice cream," she said with a laugh.

Ethan inhaled. "Wow. That smells great. What's cooking?"

Mindy looked pleased. "It's minestrone. Kind of a ritual. Every time before my ex deployed, I'd make a big batch. I heard through the grapevine that he's shipping out." She shrugged a shoulder and sighed. "I guess it's harder for me to let go than it was for Billy. He'll never be lonely. Women swarm to combat pilots like moths to porch lights. Anyway, do you want some soup? I've made a big batch because I don't know how to cook a small pot."

"We're on our way out now, but thank you for the kind offer."

Mindy nodded. "I heard sirens during the night. I wondered if there was an accident at the training."

It was no accident, he wanted to say. "Everyone is okay, but, ma'am, I have a favor to ask."

Mindy shook her head. "I'm no good with dogs."

"Don't worry. I wasn't going to ask you to dog-sit. I was going to ask if you get any more calls asking about Jillian, would you mind writing down the caller's number and letting us know?" He handed her a card. "And if you see anyone, any strangers hanging around, especially this guy, call me right away." He showed her Andy's mug shot on his phone.

A frown creased her brow. "Uh, sure. Are you thinking it's the guy from the woods that made me fall off my bike? Is he stalking Jillian?"

Ethan smiled. "We have reason to believe that he wants to hurt Jillian, but we can't prove he was in the woods. Just being cautious. Thank you, ma'am."

"You're welcome," she said. She was still frowning as she closed the door.

As soon as the bolt slid into place, Kendra turned to him.

"You've been busy. You got Andy's mug shot?"

He shrugged. "I'm not military police for nothing, you know."

"If Andy was the stranger in the woods, he won't bother calling anymore. He knows where I am. All he needs to do is wait for the right moment."

"He's not going to get the right moment, and it always pays to have a friendly neighbor watching out for you, the nosier the better."

"I'm not sure Mindy's going to be much help."

"We'll take every little bit we can get."

Kendra's cell phone rang as they returned to the kitchen. Recognizing the caller, she punched the speaker button.

"Hi, Jillian. I'm here with Ethan."

"Did you recognize the driver?" Jillian asked without preamble.

Kendra gripped the phone tighter. "No. And the plates were obscured, too."

"Yeah, I got that from Dad, but I figured maybe your memory kicked in with some other details."

"No, I couldn't see the driver's face well enough."

"She didn't drown, though," Ethan snapped. "That's a plus."

Kendra heard Jillian blow out a breath.

"I'm glad you're okay," Jillian said. "I should have started with that."

"Yeah, you should have," Ethan said under his breath. Kendra hoped Jillian hadn't heard. Then, in a louder voice, he informed Jillian, "Andy Bleakman's out of prison and skipped out on his parole officer."

There was silence on the other end of the phone for a few seconds. "Yeah? So this might be Andy going after you, not Sullivan?"

"I wish I knew," Kendra replied.

Jillian heaved a sigh. "If that creep messes up this investigation, I'll wreck him myself."

"That's good to know," Kendra said. "In the meantime, we're proceeding with the Sullivan case."

"Good. What is your next move?"

She looked at Ethan. A scowl crept over his face.

"Well…" she started.

Ethan shook his head. Should she keep things from Jillian? She wasn't sure, but Ethan was insistent. He shook his head again.

"We're chasing down a lead," she said.

"What lead?"

"I'll fill you in later."

"You'll fill me in now," Jillian said, her voice shrill. "Sullivan wants me, Kendra. I should know everything."

Ethan stepped closer to the phone. "And Kendra's standing between you and him, so you'll get the info when we have something concrete to tell you."

"My father—"

"Jillian," Ethan said, blowing out a breath and sounding suddenly weary. "Don't pull the father rank card here, okay? We are both doing everything in our power to bring Sullivan down. We want you safe, just as much as your father does."

Jillian laughed. "I thought you'd be the first one to celebrate if he took me out."

Ethan looked stricken. "No, Jillian, I wouldn't. Things were bad between us but I don't want to see you hurt. We'll call you when we've got something."

Jillian disconnected without another word.

Ethan stood, arms braced on the table, staring at the phone.

"You okay?" Kendra said, putting a hand on his shoulder. Tension made his muscles tight as steel.

"Yeah. I just... I mean... How bad did I let things get if she thinks I want her dead?"

"I'm sure she doesn't really believe that."

He closed his eyes and sighed. "She hurt me bad, yeah, but hating her is hurting me worse."

She squeezed his shoulder. "Is it time to forgive?"

He opened his eyes. "It's time to start praying for God to help me do that. I don't think I'm gonna make it on my own. Too much damage and I'm too shallow."

"I'll pray, too."

His eyes brightened like a sunlit autumn leaf and his smile touched a tender place inside her. He gazed at her until she felt she could not tear herself away.

"Thanks," he said after a moment. "I don't think I've ever had a woman pray for me besides my mother."

"I'm a newbie, like I said, but I'm making up for lost time."

He bowed his head so his lips grazed her fingers, sending sparks tripping up her arm. *No, Kendra. He doesn't want this and he doesn't want you.* She pulled away, missing the connection immediately. "Ready to go wake up your slowpoke dog?"

"Sure. Did you finish fussing over your spoiled cat?"

She huffed. "Not that it's any of your business, but I'm going to fix her a special breakfast to enjoy before we leave."

"I would expect nothing less," he said, grinning as he went to wake up Titus.

SIXTEEN

He'd arranged to meet ammo specialist Lara Dennis in an empty classroom at Canyon. They arrived with plenty of time to spare. Ethan settled Titus in the room and Kendra took a chair at the table.

Linc Colson strolled in, his rottweiler, Star, brightening when she saw Titus. He greeted Kendra politely and declined the chair Ethan offered.

"I'm on my way to a meeting but I wanted to brief you on my interview with the other suspect, Jolie Potter." He glanced at Kendra. "She's a—"

"Scientist in a biomed lab," Kendra finished.

Ethan raised an eyebrow at her.

Kendra filled them in. "I did my homework."

Ethan fought a grin. The woman had skills. "What'd you get from her, Linc?"

"Nothing substantial. They dated casually, looks like Sullivan dumped her for being too much of a brainiac."

Ethan rolled his eyes. "That figures. What a chump."

"Yeah, so most likely a dead end there. Let me know if you get anything new from Dennis."

"Will do."

Linc called to Star. "I forwarded you Sullivan's prison visitation list." His frown said it all.

"What's up?"

"There's a name on it that wasn't there before."

Ethan didn't bother to hide his shock. "How can that be?"

"You tell me."

"Name?"

"Senior Airman Chase McLear."

"No way."

Linc lifted a shoulder. "It shocked me, too. I'm just telling you what I know."

Ethan explained it to Kendra. "McLear's former Security Forces. Now he's at Canyon, raising a toddler on his own, almost done training to be a K-9 handler. He wasn't on the list when we did our initial investigation."

"Is this an official list from the prison we're talking about?" Kendra asked.

"Yes, ma'am."

She looked from Ethan to Linc. "How could McLear's name suddenly appear?"

"Question of the hour," Linc said. "This document says he visited a week before Sullivan's escape."

Frustration kicked at Ethan. "Every time I think we're making progress…"

Linc sighed. "I hear you."

"I'll arrange to meet with McLear before we leave today."

"All right." Linc left with Star.

Ethan began to pace. He didn't want to believe Chase had anything to do with Sullivan. He liked him personally, and from what he'd seen, the guy was doing a great job raising a little girl all by himself, which had to be harder than anything either of them had done on the battlefield.

Kendra eyed him. "The pacing's not going to help, you know."

"It might."

"It just makes Titus go bug-eyed trying to watch your every move."

He stopped. It was probably agitating Titus as she said, and the dog had been through enough. Besides, fatigue from Ethan's wrestling match with the river bogged him down, too. "Gonna get coffee. May I get you some?"

She lit up like a string of Christmas lights and his stomach got a weird flutter. "I would adore a cup of coffee, you wonderful man."

He laughed. "And I thought you admired my killer MP skills. Turns out I could have just impressed you with a cup of coffee."

"I'm already impressed, but the coffee gets you extra points."

"Coming right up." He went to the vending machine, whistling as he went. Already impressed? It felt good, he could not deny it, to have Kendra think well of him. That thought both thrilled and scared him. *You care too much what she thinks. Just get the coffee and do your job, Webb.*

At the vending machine, he found former combat pilot Isaac Goddard collecting his own cup of joe. Shadows smudged Isaac's eyes. Clearly, combat did not come without a price and Isaac had paid it many times over. Getting help for his PTSD was the first step. Bringing home the dog who saved his life was the second. Beacon had kept him alive, though his handler, Isaac's good friend Jake Burke, did not survive. Ethan wondered what would happen to Isaac if bringing Beacon home proved impossible.

"Hey, Isaac."

He looked up, his green eyes hazy for a moment. "Hey, Ethan. I heard you found one of the missing dogs."

"Yeah. Little Malinois pup."

"Gonna be okay?"

"He's improving daily from what I hear from Westley." He considered whether or not to bring up Beacon, but one thing he'd despised about his return after combat was people treating him like an egg, as if he might crack at any moment. So he asked the question.

"Any word on Beacon?"

Isaac frowned. "He's been spotted in enemy territory. Guy from my outfit's been trying to lure him over, but no success yet."

"I'll keep up the prayers."

Isaac blew out a breath. "Yeah. Thanks."

Ethan imagined for a moment what it would be like to lose Titus. He'd lost a dog before, and it burned like wildfire, but at least he knew what had happened. There was grieving and closure. Thinking about Titus running loose, scared, injured…? He shook the thought away and returned to the conference room. He handed Kendra the coffee just as a small woman with her long hair pulled back into a tight bun entered the room. Her hands were fisted before she snapped off a salute.

Ethan returned the salute. "Thank you for coming. Specialist Lara Dennis, right?"

"Yes, Lieutenant," she said, shooting a quick glance at Kendra.

"I'm Jillian Masters," Kendra said. "I'm helping Ethan with the investigation."

Dennis's eyes shifted between them. "Isn't he your ex-husband?"

Kendra nodded. "Yes, but we're getting remarried soon."

The word *married* jolted him. It had taken him countless painful days to accept the label of "ex-husband," a title that reminded him just how gullible he had been.

After a blink he said, "Please sit down." He offered a smile that she did not return.

"All due respect, I'd prefer to stand, Lieutenant."

Was she sending him a defiant message or just nervous? "All right. Just a few quick questions and we'll get you on the road. Tell me again about your relationship with Boyd Sullivan."

She didn't react. She'd been expecting the question, of course. Why else would she be summoned? Still he caught the tightening of her mouth.

"I've already told the investigation team everything. I…I was attracted to Sullivan when we were going through basic. We had lunch together, we talked. That's it."

"I don't think so," Kendra said.

Dennis stared. "Yes, it is."

Kendra didn't say anything, only stared. Ethan knew the tactic and he remained silent also. If Kendra sensed there was something deeper, he'd go with her instincts.

Dennis's gaze fell to her boots. "I… It took me a while to realize what kind of guy he was. He wanted more, another date, I didn't. I declined any further contact with him and he was horrible about it. End of story."

"Why didn't you like him?" Kendra said.

Dennis started, "I… He was the center of his own universe, ma'am. I liked the confidence at first, or I thought I did, but there's a difference between confidence you earn and confidence you have no business with. You get the difference, ma'am?"

Kendra nodded.

"How was he horrible when you brushed him off, exactly?" Ethan said.

Her lips thinned. "Phoning me all the time, sending flowers, alternately begging and then calling me names and then apologizing. He wasn't...stable."

"Yet you didn't complain to your CO?"

Her gaze dropped to her lap. "No, sir."

"Why not? That's protocol for harassment."

Dennis remained quiet, her hands clenched.

"I think I can answer that," Kendra said. "Tell me if I get anything wrong. You didn't tell your CO because you worked hard to get where you are, a woman in a man's profession. You're raising a child, a son, by yourself, and you put yourself through high school at nights, working days, passed all the basic training and Airmen's Week plus the National Agency Check and Local Agency checks. You've worked harder for this than anything else in your life and you didn't want the possible stigma attached to a messy relationship with a guy you could kick yourself for even giving a second look." Kendra raised an eyebrow. "Am I close?"

Kendra had done her homework on Lara Dennis.

Dennis swallowed. "Yes, ma'am. I just want it to be over and get on with my life, take care of my boy and make him proud of me. I messed up a lot as a teen and this is the first time I've made something good for both of us. I can't jeopardize that, not for Sullivan or anyone else." The look she gave Kendra was pleading. "Do you understand, ma'am?"

"Yes," Kendra said quietly. "I understand completely."

A guy she could kick herself for even giving a second look.

Unstable.

Yes, he realized. Kendra did understand.

Ethan stood outside the moment, watching two strong women who'd never met make a connection because of the lives they'd chosen and the consequences they hadn't. The strength of it stopped him, the grace of it.

He forced himself back to the task. "Have you had any further contact with Boyd Sullivan since?"

"No, sir, and that is the honest truth."

He looked at Kendra who gave him a slight nod. "All right. Thank you for coming in. We appreciate your time." They exchanged salutes.

Dennis walked to the door, stopping before she crossed the threshold.

"Ma'am, if I may," she said, looking at Kendra.

Kendra nodded at her to continue.

"Ma'am, Sullivan used to talk about people who crossed him. He said that no one would get away with humiliating him." She twisted her cap in her hands. "Uh, I've heard talk and all, that you cut him down pretty good in front of his friends."

"Say what you need to say, Dennis," Ethan said.

One final wring of her cap and she plunged in. "He's not going to forget, ma'am. He's that kind of person and he'll be carrying that grudge until the day he dies."

"Or until we put him in prison again," Ethan said.

"Just saying, ma'am," Dennis said. "He won't forget."

Again a look passed between them, something that spoke of the instant bond they'd formed. "Thank you, Dennis."

"You're welcome, sir, ma'am. I hope you get him."

"We will," Ethan said, eyes on Kendra. "We will."

SEVENTEEN

Private eyes and MPs had a lot of duties in common, Kendra thought. Limited glamour but plenty of legwork and reports to complete. After four phone calls, Ethan discovered that Chase McLear was off base for the day, but he managed to get him to agree to meet at a coffee shop in a town a couple hours outside of Canyon. They walked to the truck, the sun blazing at just before noon.

More coffee was fine by Kendra. Her body felt like it had been put through a violent wash cycle and chucked against some sharp rocks to dry. She was physically wrung out, but worse was the emotional upheaval that churned below the surface. The tasks of the day were all that was keeping her from reliving every terrible moment of her plunge into the creek. On top of that, their lack of progress chafed.

Had they accomplished anything at all with their most recent visit to Canyon? Lara Dennis was a dead end, she was sure of it, and the scientist, no more promising. Yvette Crenville, the base nutritionist, had been interviewed several times to no avail. Kendra was straining to muster further possibilities when Heidi Jenks caught up to them.

Ethan stood taller, tension visible in the set of his jaw.

"Jillian," she said. "I heard about what happened after I left the drill. Are you all right?"

"Yes. Thanks."

She waited for the inevitable and the reporter did not disappoint her.

"Would you be interested in talking a bit about your experience?"

"No."

"It might help the investigation, you know, to get more information out there about Sullivan's accomplice." She lowered her voice. "I heard it might be a woman who tried to run you down."

"How'd you hear that exactly, Jenks?" Ethan demanded.

She glared at him. "I have contacts, Ethan, that's my job. People are always willing to talk eventually."

"Not me," Kendra said. "I have no comment now or ever."

Jenks sighed. "Okay. If you change your mind, let me know."

"I'm sure none of the details will wind up on the underground blog, right?" Ethan's tone was acid.

Jenks stared right back at him. "I wouldn't know, Ethan. I told you, that isn't me. Whoever's leaking information isn't reporting, they're gossiping."

He snorted. "And you don't do that?"

"No," she said. "No matter what you think about me, I'm a reporter and I take my duty seriously. I have a job to do, just like the two of you, and I'm going to do it with or without your cooperation." Turning on her heel, she stalked away.

"You trust her?" Ethan said.

"I don't know. She was there at the drill, she knew the details of the exercise. She had plenty of time to leave and make plans to run me down, but she has no connection to Boyd Sullivan."

"That we know of," he said darkly.

They got in the car and drove off. With the air conditioner cranked to high, the truck gradually cooled and Kendra logged on to her email to check for any new info.

"Andy's still not using his car or his credit cards, as far as I can tell," she said.

A movement behind them caught both their attention. Ethan stared into the rearview mirror. "Black car, tinted windows at our six o'clock."

"I see it," she said, staring into the side-view mirror.

"Changed lanes to stay with us, two cars back."

"I saw that, too."

"Can you get plates?"

She squinted into the side mirror, making a note in her phone. "Got it."

He handed her his phone. "Text it to Linc. Have him run the plate numbers."

She did. "He said to give him a minute."

Ethan continued on, keeping pace with the flow of traffic. Kendra could not get a good look at the driver. Goose bumps prickled her skin and she could recall the roaring of the engine as the driver came at her on the bridge, aiming for a kill. Possible suspects clicked through her mind. Sullivan? His female accomplice? Andy? Her palms were slick as she gripped the phone, the minutes stretching along with the miles until she thought she would scream. *It's like a combat zone, with potential enemies around every corner.*

The phone buzzed. She read the details from Linc's message aloud to Ethan.

"The car belongs to a real estate agent, Louis Bickford. No ties to Baylor or Canyon that Linc can see."

Kendra deflated, sagging against the seat. Frustration edged out over relief.

Ethan groaned. "Do you think we're getting paranoid?"

Was she? The familiar tightness squeezed her belly. She bit her lip, staring out the window as the black car gradually eased back into the flow of traffic.

"Hey," Ethan said, startling her by taking her hand. "You drifted away there for a minute. Did I say something wrong?"

"No." She swallowed. "It's just…my mom had severe paranoia, exacerbated by her addiction, before she was hospitalized full-time. It…hurt, when she turned that paranoia on me." She could still hear her mother's screams from her hospital bed. *Get her away from me. She hates me. She wants to kill me.* Her mother's rejection had ripped open such a gaping hole, leaving Kendra vulnerable to Andy, and seeking alcohol and drugs to fill it.

"Aw, man," he said. "I'm sorry. Let me just try to pry my boot out of my big mouth."

She squeezed his fingers. "There's no way you could have known." Her eyes drifted to the scarf still rolled up on the floor. "I think Mom tried her best, but she was sick and addicted. It was hard not to take it personally, though, especially when I was younger, but I've grown. I understand now. People have flaws, big ones."

"But it still hurts."

She heaved a sigh. "Yeah, it hurts, but I think God's going to make something good out of it."

"How?" His brown eyes were so warm and sincere, she found herself articulating it aloud.

"It came to me as we talked to Lara Dennis about her son. For a long while, I thought I would never have kids because I didn't want to risk breaking their hearts like my mother broke mine, but you know what?" A spark of new hope danced inside her. "I think I'm going to be a better mother because I know how hard that job is, and how incredibly important, like Lara Dennis does."

He looked as though she'd slapped him. "Ethan? I think it's my turn for a boot in the mouth. What did I say?"

"Ah, it was a bone of contention between me and Jillian." His face flushed. "I really wanted kids and she told me she did, too, so every month after I thought we'd started trying, I'd get my hopes up." He shrugged. "She just gave it lip service, never intended to have children, not with me anyway."

"Then she's crazy." She couldn't stop blurting out the words.

He didn't seem to hear. "I decided a guy who couldn't tell that his own wife was lying to him probably wasn't good father material. I'm not going to have a family." He forced a smile that didn't reach his eyes. "Gonna stick to dogs."

She clasped his hand between hers. "Like I said, He uses that stuff for good. Jillian's betrayal and my enormous mess-ups and everything. Don't focus on the rearview, right?"

For a moment, he looked at her, eyes shimmering, as if he was probing in search of some answer he keenly wanted. Then he squeezed her fingers again and pulled his hands away, his face expressionless behind the handsome mask.

"I learned my lesson," he mumbled. "I'll leave it at that."

She'd made him uncomfortable by mentioning children. Yes, he was working on letting go of the hatred for his ex-wife, but the damage would take a long time, maybe a lifetime, to overcome. It dragged her heart down and she ached for him. As the miles silently wore on, she lost herself in the beat of the country music.

Bless the broken road.

That led me to you.

Thank You, God, for the broken road that led me to Ethan Webb, she prayed inside. The prayer was automatic and she knew in the deep places that they would not travel that road together much longer. But for now, for the moment. with the warm sun and the snoring dog and Ethan's strong profile and the purple scarf at her feet, she thanked Him.

Ethan gripped the wheel, pulling into the parking lot of a coffee shop, and parked in the shade.

From the back seat the dog gave a might yawn.

"Titus is coffee shop approved?"

"He goes where I go. End of story." He scoped out the outdoor seating area. "I'm gonna sit him in the shade, grab a table away from everyone else. Want to get us some coffee?" He reached for his wallet.

"You have to ask? Don't worry. It's on me. A stall tactic until I buy you and Titus that steak dinner."

He chuckled. "You make me laugh, and that's a rare gift in this world."

She smiled, realizing that it had been a long time since she'd shared laughter with a good man. A rare gift, for sure. Sullivan would be caught, and she would track down Andy Bleakman on her own. Once the case was closed, their time together would end. The laughter would be only a memory. So be it. She'd savor each chuckle and smile, storing them carefully away in her memory.

The twinge of sadness remained as she pushed past the coffee shop door.

* * *

Ethan faced Chase McLear. McLear's green eyes took in every detail, the space, exits, entrances, everything a former Security Forces guy would notice. He gave Kendra a long look.

"She's not leaving my side until Sullivan is caught," Ethan said, by way of explanation. "You've heard about the threats."

McLear played with his coffee cup. "I can't believe we're even having this conversation. You know I had nothing to do with Sullivan. I'm minding my own business, training my dog. This is crazy and you know it."

Ethan thought so, too. McLear and Queenie, his beagle, were almost through their sessions and Queenie would be one of the first dogs ever to be qualified as an electronic sniffer at Canyon. McLear was also the single father to young Allie after her mother had abandoned the child.

But he needed to keep his emotions out of this investigation.

"I don't want to be here any more than you do, but your name is on the prison list. You visited Sullivan."

Chase put the cup down hard, splashing coffee over the edge, each word sharp as a blade. "I did not."

"Can you explain why your name's on the list?"

"I can't." He grimaced. "But one Security Forces guy to another, if I were you, I'd be coming to two possible conclusions."

Ethan watched for any sign that McLear was lying, a change in the timbre of his voice, a sideways glance, an unusual gesture. He saw only confusion and mounting frustration. "Do my work for me then, Chase. What are my two theories?"

McLear rolled his coffee cup between his palms. "First

theory. I did visit Sullivan because I'm his accomplice. Maybe I paid off a prison staffer to keep my name off the list, but I refused to keep paying off said staffer and he or she corrected the record."

"Good theory," Ethan said. "What's the second?"

"That someone is trying to frame me, to throw suspicion off themselves."

"And to which theory do you ascribe?"

McLear scowled. "What do you think?"

Kendra stood and walked to the trash can to throw her paper napkin away.

"Ethan, this isn't some adventure story here. This is my life," McLear said. "And my kid's life."

"You don't have to tell me that," Ethan snapped. "There are a lot of lives at stake."

Kendra's for one. He glanced her way again, noticing the way the sun burnished her hair into copper fire. She brushed a flyaway strand back, her attention drawn by something.

McLear smacked the table, claiming his attention. "Ethan, someone is manipulating the evidence and this investigation. I'm not guilty of anything and you know it."

"I don't know anything right now, Chase, but I'm gonna find out, I promise."

McLear started to answer when Kendra called Ethan. He turned to her and when he saw her expression, he hurried to her side. Titus scrambled after him. The patrons gave the dog a wide berth.

"Isn't that the car?" she whispered, craning her neck toward the parking lot.

He followed her gaze to the black car, the one that he'd thought had been following them earlier. Coincidence? There weren't very many coffee shops convenient to the freeway here. Maybe the Realtor had stopped, too. But Ethan knew there were not too many coincidences in combat zones, either, only missed clues that got a person dead.

"Kendra, stay here, I'm going to—"

His words were drowned out by the crash of breaking glass.

EIGHTEEN

In a blur, Kendra saw Ethan catapult down the landing into the parking lot, Titus keeping pace at his heels. The sound came from under the trees where Ethan's truck was parked next to an older model Mercedes. Across from the two vehicles was the black sedan they'd had Linc trace earlier, empty, as far as Kendra could tell.

She heard the sound of more shattering glass, then the thwack of a blunt object against metal.

Racing after Ethan, hand on her gun, she yelled at a patron to call the cops and hit the blacktop, sprinting. Zeroing in on the noise, she saw bits of broken glass sparkling through the air as a man—Caucasian, medium height, wearing a baseball cap pulled low on his brow—brought a tire iron down on the windshield of Ethan's truck.

Ethan shouted as he closed in and the man flung down the tire iron and hurtled into the driver's seat of the Mercedes, the engine already running.

She caught up just as Ethan leaped at the door of the Mercedes, which the driver had not had time to close fully. Titus jumped up at the back windows, scratching and clawing as the driver gunned the engine, headed for the parking lot exit. Kendra's fingers itched to fire at the rear tires, but with Ethan and Titus so close, she didn't dare.

With a grunt of frustration, Titus bounced off the car, rolling once and springing to all fours again. Undeterred, he again started to chase after the car and Ethan, his legs churning into blurs of brown fur. Ethan managed to wrench the door open and reach in to grab the driver.

Her heart soared. Finally. They would have something tangible, someone to interrogate. A fist struck out and punched Ethan in the jaw, sending him flying onto the pavement, where he tumbled over twice, coming to rest on his back. The car roared away onto the main street, out of sight in a matter of moments.

A patron raced up, a phone to his ear, blinking incredulously. "That's my Mercedes. That guy just stole my car."

"Hot-wired it," another said. "Had it running the whole time while he bashed in some guy's windows. What a looney."

Kendra holstered her weapon and ran to Ethan, stopping a few feet away to avoid Titus's frenzy. The dog pranced around him, darting licks and whining, barking savagely at anyone who got close to Ethan. She tried speaking calmly to the dog, but her voice did not penetrate. He was all teeth and claws, determined that no one was going to approach his fallen partner.

At last Ethan propped himself on his elbows, breathing hard. "It's all right," he panted. "At ease, boy." Titus was unconvinced until he all but sat in Ethan's lap, slathering him with a wet tongue and poking a nose into his face. Gradually, after more soothing from Ethan, the dog calmed enough that Kendra could get near.

"Are you all right?"

"Yeah," he said, sitting up and rubbing his jaw. "I

would have got him if I had better leverage." He caressed the dog, massaging his quivering sides. "I know, boy. I should have let you go first. You'd have gotten him." Ethan's forehead was scratched, his chin smudged with dirt, but he wasn't hurt, not badly, and Titus was in a state of bliss, legs sprawled in every direction as he did his best to be a lapdog.

Tousling the dog's floppy ears, Ethan ordered him to a sit, which he reluctantly obeyed, never taking his eyes off his handler.

Kendra helped Ethan to a standing position. He leaned on her, his chin brushing the top of her head. She circled his waist, holding him close, secretly grateful that there had been no shots fired. They hadn't gotten their man, but for the moment, she couldn't care too much about that. She held on tight, willing herself not to think, just to feel Ethan's solid presence in her arms, the steady beat of his heart, the Southern drawl echoing in her ears.

"I'm okay," he said.

And it was truly all that mattered in that moment.

"Cops are on their way," McLear said, trotting up. "You okay, man?"

They stepped back from each other. "Just bounced around is all. The black car must have been recently stolen. That's why Linc's earlier search didn't trigger the info. Owner probably doesn't even realize it's missing yet."

"He's got a new set of wheels now, since he just stole the Mercedes. I relayed the plate info to the cops," McLear said. "Looks like you're going to need a new vehicle, too."

Ethan sucked in a breath. The front windshield was bashed to pieces, a hole punched through the safety glass and the driver's window shattered.

Kendra clamped her lips together when she saw the rest. Sprayed in orange paint across the hood of his truck was a phone number.

The dripping numbers made her skin crawl. A taunt, from a man so angry or so desperate that he'd risk everything to deliver his message in broad daylight in a very public place. Who was that kind of desperate? Sullivan? She cast a glance at McLear. He could have tipped off Sullivan about their meeting place. All the concern on his face might just be acting, pure and simple. Suspicions whirled around in her mind, dizzying. Too many suspects. Too few solid leads.

With a look of unadulterated fury, Ethan yanked his phone from his pocket and dialed the number sprayed on his truck, stepping away from the bystanders into the shade of the trees. She followed and he put the phone on speaker.

"Let's talk," Ethan growled when someone picked up. "Who is this?"

"Hello, G.I. Joe. Too bad about your truck," a man said.

Kendra's heart stuttered to a stop. It was a voice she would never forget, a voice rooted deep in her memories and nightmares.

You'll do what I say because you love me.

You'll do what I say.

Or you'll die.

From the corner of her memory she heard Baby's terrified mewing, her own harsh breathing, the sound of a knife yanked from its leather sheath, the muffled slam of a terrified heart beating against quaking ribs.

"Identify yourself," Ethan said. "Or aren't you man enough?"

He laughed. "Why don't you ask Kendra? I know she's

there with you. I've been watching her play soldier. Working on a case now that you're a fancy PI and all, Kendra?"

Ethan looked at Kendra. Her mouth went dry and she could not produce one single syllable.

I've been watching.

Every nerve, every atom was slowly icing over, freezing her from the inside out.

"Come on, baby," Andy crooned. "It's been a while and I'm dying to hear your voice. I know you're looking forward to seeing me again, aren't you?"

Her brain had known he was close, circling like a shark, but hearing his voice was a nightmare come to life, as if she could feel the nip of razor-sharp teeth as they prepared to rip into her, severing her body, devouring her a piece at a time.

"Andy…" she whispered.

"There you are, Kendra," Andy said. "I knew I'd find you. Piece of cake after I figured out where Jillian lived."

Find you.

She wanted to scream. It could not be real. She could not be powerless again.

"Time to settle some things, don't you think?" Andy said.

One cell at a time her body turned to ice.

Well past time, she thought.

Ethan held the phone in a death grip. "Bleakman," he grunted through his teeth. "Why are we talking on the phone? Not man enough to stand up to me in person? You smash up my truck and run away like a scared rabbit?"

"Listen, G.I. Joe. This isn't your business. This is between me and Kendra."

"I'm making it my business. Drive on back here right now and we'll settle it."

There was a pause, a long one, long enough for Ethan to feel the stampeding blood in his veins, the bone-cracking tension in his muscles, the overwhelming need to punish Andy Bleakman, to grind him under his boot like a poisonous scorpion.

"So it's like that, huh, Kendra?" Bleakman said. "You left me to rot in jail while you moved on with G.I. Joe here?"

"No," Kendra said. "That's not it."

"Doesn't matter," Ethan barked. "You're not gonna terrorize her, not gonna lay one finger on her, you hear me?"

"Kendra needs to pay her debt, G.I. Joe. Everyone has to pay." The background traffic noise revealed him to be on the freeway. He mouthed the info to Kendra, watched her text the info to Linc, who would funnel it to the police. He didn't trust that McLear would do it, didn't trust anyone at the moment.

"And you know what?" Bleakman said. "Anyone who gets in my way is going to pay the price, too."

"Easy to spout threats on the phone," Ethan told him. "Be a man. Come and face me."

"What a good soldier, just like my old man. Sheep, all of you. Follow orders and do what you're told, a grunt to the end."

Ethan breathed hard. "Where are you, Bleakman? Stop running, coward."

Another laugh, low and slow. "I'm done talking to you, Soldier. You're dismissed, so toddle along like a good little grunt and take your dog for a walk. Kendra," he said and Ethan could hear a smile in the tone. "I'll see you soon. Very soon."

The connection went dead.

He pocketed the phone, noting the color fade out of

Kendra's cheeks. The rapid rise and fall of her chest made him reach for her.

"Maybe you should…" He was going to say "sit down" but she was already turning away, wrestling a phone from her pocket.

"Who are you calling?"

"First the tow company," she said, no quiver in the voice.

"Second?"

"I need to tell Jillian that Andy's definitely in town." She hesitated, her troubled eyes locked on his. "Andy will hurt anyone who gets between me and him. Including Jillian…and you."

He edged in front of her, fighting the urge to crush her to his chest. "I hope he does make a move, Kendra, because I'm going to take him down."

Now he saw her tears sparkling like morning dew before the sun, and her body shook all over. "I don't want anybody hurt," she whispered. "Especially you." He went to her then and she let the phone drop to her side. For a while he held her, wrapped in his arms, and murmured comforting words into her ear.

"We're going to get him, Kendra."

She jerked and tried to back away but he held on.

"No. No more 'we,'" she whispered, her eyes feverish. "I can't allow it."

He cupped her chin in his hand, preventing her from escaping, willing her to listen. "I know what you're thinking and stop it right now. We're going to get him together, just like Sullivan. No lone wolf here, no John Wayne action."

A flicker of a smile. "Says the guy with the accent and the rifle."

He kissed her, on the corner of her mouth, drinking

in the soft scent of her, the strength and delicacy, the marvel. For a moment he was swept into another place where he could love again, a place where his heart was not in pieces.

"Kendra," he started. The luscious brown of her eyes drew him, beckoned him to trust. What would happen if he did?

While he wrestled with the question, she answered it by moving away. The inches between them spoke volumes. She was ready for kids, a healthy relationship built with a man who could trust and love and forgive. He'd shown her he was not that man.

"We have a job to do," she said.

He stared, tried to absorb the unspoken.

"The cops," she continued. "They're here."

"Okay." He swallowed hard. He understood what he wasn't saying. She didn't want to go to that place with him. Maybe she might have earlier. He thought he'd felt that in her embrace after she'd nearly drowned, and again the moment at the kitchen table over omelets. But he'd let the moments pass out of fear and now she'd put up a wall, invisible but impenetrable. She was right anyway. It wasn't the time nor the place.

He watched her go to the cop. "You let that chance slip away," he told himself. Only the job stood before him now, duty, purpose, meaning.

Get Sullivan. Get Andy and get on with your life, Ethan.

NINETEEN

Kendra forced her fears into a tight ball and shoved it down deep. Uncertainty clawed at her. She was not sure how to proceed, how to both escape Andy and capture Sullivan, but she knew one thing for certain: she could not allow Ethan to get hurt because of her sordid past. And he would.

Andy wasn't bluffing when he said he would destroy anyone who got in his way. He'd beaten senseless a man in prison who'd bumped his lunch tray. A savage, with a hair-trigger temper. How stupid she'd been not to see it sooner. She deserved to pay the price for getting tangled up with him, but Ethan did not.

They finished with the police and waited for a tow truck. Ethan's look was mournful as he surveyed the damage. He ran his hand over the hood. "Aw, Big Mac. Just look at you."

She smothered a giggle.

He gave her a sheepish look. "Don't you name your cars?"

"Well, no."

"This truck is special. Bought it when I was seventeen." He gave it one final pat. "Don't you worry, Big Mac. Gonna get you all fixed up."

It would take a chunk out of his salary, depending what the insurance supplied, to have the glass and body work done and the repainting on the old truck. All because of Andy. Her fingernails bit into her palms.

Ethan stopped the driver just before he drove away with the wrecked truck. He retrieved the scarf his mother made for him, quickly shaking out the glass and shoving it in his pocket, probably hoping no one was looking. She pretended not to notice but it stirred her inside. Ethan Webb was a good man. He'd make someone an excellent husband someday if he could accept who he was and forgive himself and Jillian. She fought a sudden lump in her throat.

They rented an SUV with room for Titus in the back, and as they drove, both of them constantly checked the rearview mirror to be sure Andy wasn't following. Every black vehicle made her breath quicken until she considered that Andy might have already stolen another car, since he knew the police had the plate number of the Mercedes.

They finally pulled up at Jillian's house. It was evening now, the heat giving way to a wind that blew in the clouds and promised another storm. Kendra's legs felt like they were made of cement as she dragged herself to the front porch.

"Stay here a minute," Ethan ordered.

Too tired to protest his bossiness, she waited on the mat until he and Titus had checked every square inch of the house.

"All clear," he said as his phone pinged. Kendra could hear the colonel's anger clearly as Ethan held the phone slightly away from his ear.

"Yes, Colonel Masters, I can confirm it was Andy

Bleakman." Ethan shot a look at her. "It's a…situation from her past."

More angry ranting from the colonel.

"We're both tired, and we need to discuss strategy tonight. We'll brief you on base tomorrow afternoon."

Ethan winced and she heard the accent creep deeper into his conversation along with a dark stain on his cheeks. "That will have to do, Colonel. I don't work for you, remember? So if you wanna demote me, take it up with the air force."

He disconnected.

"He has a right to be angry," she said as they entered the house. "I didn't tell him about Andy when I took the Sullivan case."

"He's always angry whether he has a right to be or not. Your past is your business, not his."

"You shouldn't jeopardize your career."

"Like I said, Masters is not my boss."

"But he can make trouble for you."

He gave her a cocky grin. "I can handle it. Trouble is my middle name. Ethan William Trouble Webb."

"Rolls right off the tongue."

"You got that right, ma'am."

That charm, the sincerity, inched their way into her heart again. She heard his stomach growl.

"Up for some early dinner?" he said. "I can make a mean spaghetti."

Her heart said yes, but the fear still circled down deep and her conscience pricked her. *You need a plan to keep Ethan away from Andy.* "I want to be alone for a while, to think." She scooped Baby from the floor and stroked her.

"All right. As long as that doesn't mean planning to go after Andy without me."

His eyes bored into her, but she kept her attention on

Baby. "I'm doing nothing until the morning. That's the best I can promise."

He huffed and folded his arms across his middle. "You're not doing this alone, Kendra. Not anymore."

"I made the mess. I have to clean it up." *Because I would never forgive myself if something happened to you.*

"It's my job to help you."

My job. She wondered why the words hurt. He'd never said anything, never even hinted that he wanted something else from her, no false promises, just a pledge to do his duty. As a matter of fact, he'd fought hard against working together in the first place. His job. She would leave him to his duty, and she would do hers. It was easier, better for both of them.

"I'm tired, Ethan. I want to lie down for a while. Can we talk more in later?"

He held her gaze for a moment more. "All right. I'll check the yard one more time before I go to my unit. Your phone charged?"

"I'll make sure."

"Titus and I are going to do a few patrols throughout the night."

"You don't—" She realized the futility of what she was about to argue. Duty.

"Gotta keep the skills up," he said with a grin.

She pointed to Titus. "His or yours?"

Ethan huffed. "My skills are sharp as a good cheddar."

"I feel safer already."

He laughed. "Should have come up with something better than a cheese analogy, but I'm tired, too."

She carried Baby to the bedroom and took a shower, pulled on some fatigues and tried to read, with no success. She knew she should be resting, but hearing Andy's voice had stripped all her normal senses away, leaving only the naked pulse of fear.

She went to the window, looking out into the yard now filling up with shadows. A light shone in Ethan's unit, a pinprick of gold against the gloom. Wind riffled through the branches of the trees in the woods that bordered the property. Was Andy out there now? Watching? Biding his time?

Forcing away the notion, she pulled the curtains closed tight and checked that her weapon was loaded and ready.

Ethan didn't have to work hard to wake Titus for their first check at midnight. The dog seemed to be sleeping as fitfully as his owner. "Patrol," he said and Titus offered the little wiggly rump dance while Ethan zipped on his harness.

He let them out quietly. The smell of rain hung heavy in the air, which would not pose a problem for Titus unless it came down in buckets. Light rain would actually refresh any human scent and he felt confident that Titus would alert if he got a trail on a stranger hiding anywhere near the house. He let the dog have his lead and followed him around the perimeter, flashlight on to pick up any broken foliage or footprints.

When Titus whined and sat, he drew his weapon, until he realized it was Kendra watching him from the bedroom window.

"Goofball," he said to his dog. Titus flapped his ears.

Kendra slid open the window.

"Can't sleep?" he said.

"No. Want company?"

He wanted her company, craved it to be truthful, though he told himself it was foolish. "Better for you to stay in the house."

"I need fresh air."

"But—"

She'd already vanished from the window. He sighed. "She doesn't listen any better than her cat," he told Titus.

The dog offered a wide yawn.

Kendra joined them in a few minutes wearing fatigues and armed, he was glad to see. She trailed along behind Ethan and Titus, careful to stay out of their way. She smelled of some fruity shampoo. He felt something inside slide into place, some jagged piece that seemed to find a spot to belong, and he realized it was because she was near him. He sped up, but the thoughts kept pace. He did not want a relationship, not now, so why did his emotions refuse to get the message? The clouds obscured the moon, and the porch light that they'd left on cast a glow that accentuated her resemblance to Jillian.

Remember that, Ethan? You thought Jillian was your missing piece, too. You were an idiot then, giving your heart away without the consent of your brain. And what had it cost him? Everything, his pride, his self-confidence, his future. He wasn't ready for a relationship with Kendra, or anyone else. Period.

Titus completed his perimeter check and they moved onto the yard. There were very few places a person might hide, but Titus checked every inch anyway, behind the shed, along the fence line, stopping at the back gate. He whined, pawing at the metal gate. Ethan's adrenaline went through the roof.

"Go back in the house, Kendra. Wait for my text. If you don't hear from me in twenty, call the cops." He pushed the gate open, Titus barreling through.

"I'm coming."

"No, you're not."

"You're not facing Andy alone if he's out there."

"Kendra," he snapped.

She lifted her chin, eyes blazing. "Unless you're going to handcuff me to the fence, get moving, Lieutenant."

Smothering an angry retort, he pushed out into the woods, fuming. If Titus was alerting to Andy, he would take care of it without risking Kendra's life. He was an MP, after all. Did she think he needed her to back him up? Think him a pushover like Jillian had?

Titus yanked and pulled and Ethan worked to keep up and not trip over any fallen branches or rocks. Kendra shadowed them easily.

Ethan was puzzled. Titus did not seem to be latching onto a scent and following it to a potential intruder's hiding place, as he did in his patrol duties. Something about the dog's erratic behavior was atypical. He thought about stopping him and resetting, but Titus was wired, filled with frantic energy. *Trust your dog*, his gut told him.

"What is it, boy?" Titus did not acknowledge Ethan, his nose glued to the ground, the hair on his back raised.

"What's he after?" Kendra whispered.

"I don't know," he whispered back. "Titus, if you're dragging me around these woods looking for a squirrel, you're grounded forever."

The dog whined, swiveling from one side of a grassy basin to another. The area was clear of trees, a jumble of rocks off to one side, glittering with moisture. Titus beelined to the rocks. He pawed, sniffed, pawed again. To Ethan's utter shock, the dog turned a circle and lay down, head on his paws.

Ethan gaped.

"What?" Kendra said. "What is he alerting on? Nobody's here."

The words seemed to come from far away. "Nobody alive," Ethan said.

Her eyes widened. "Are you saying…"

"That's the signal he's supposed to use to tell me he's discovered human remains." Her shock mirrored his own.

Almost imperceptibly at first, the rain began to fall, cold droplets that he did not feel. Titus put his head on his paws and let out a long, mournful whine.

TWENTY

The morning finally dawned, poking feebly through the rain clouds. Kendra was chilled, both inside and out, from the night in the woods as Carpenter led his team to clear the rocks to reveal whatever Titus had detected.

Ethan's words circled in her memory. *Nobody alive.*

She prayed the dog was mistaken, but deep down she knew he wasn't.

The county coroner was leading the proceedings, a yellow slicker keeping the rain off. She and Ethan watched from under the cover of pine trees, Titus whining and bumping Ethan's leg.

"Easy, boy," Ethan said. "He's never alerted on a cadaver before except for our drills. I'm not sure why he's so agitated."

It wasn't a stretch for Kendra. Her nerves were strung to the breaking point, too, as the police dug, photographed, dug some more, brushed the debris away and repeated the process. It was time-consuming and laborious but Kendra was touched at the respect the officers showed to the victim.

When the remains were finally exhumed from the hole, Kendra gasped.

"It isn't… I mean, that didn't happen recently."

Ethan looped an arm around her. "No. Looks like the body has been there for a while, a couple of months at least."

"More than eight months, I would speculate," the coroner piped up. He talked into a tape recorder as he took samples and made measurements. Using the tip of a pen, he lifted something off the female victim and held it to the light. A filigree earring that glittered in the beam.

"I…I thought it was Andy's work," Kendra said, "but he was in prison. But it couldn't be Sullivan either could it? He was in jail too until his escape two months ago."

Ethan grimaced. "Right."

"What is going on?"

They turned to find Mindy, dressed in jeans and a sweatshirt, one curler still clinging to her hair, an umbrella over her head. "I heard all the noise." Her gaze went to the grisly bundle. "Is that…?"

"A body," said Officer Carpenter. "And we need to keep this area clear, okay? Ms. Zeppler, isn't it? I'll be asking you some questions later, but for now, I'd like to ask you to return to your house and not alert anyone. We need to finish our work here."

Mindy took a faltering step back, her palm pressed to her heart. When Ethan reached out to steady her, Titus yanked the leash from his grip and bolted.

"Titus," Ethan roared, but the dog flew over the carpet of pine needles.

"Dog, you're in such bad trouble I can't even begin to describe it," Ethan hollered as he ran.

"Where's he going?" Mindy blurted. "Is someone out there? A killer?"

Kendra reassured her neighbor. "Everything's okay, Mindy. The police have it all under control. Go straight home, like they said, okay?"

"I'll send an officer to escort you," Carpenter said.

Her mouth pinched, Mindy hugged herself and walked quickly back in the direction of her house with an officer. As soon as Kendra was sure Mindy was headed away from the horrible scene, she took off in pursuit of Ethan and Titus.

The woods seemed to close around her, shutting off the sound of the police activity. Dripping leaves and rustling branches played havoc with her nerves. How long had the woods kept the secret of the dead woman? Who was she? There must have been someone looking for her, wondering and mourning, praying each day that she would be discovered. Bile rose in her throat.

Forcing in some air to combat the nausea, she took a path up, pushing by shrubs that reached out to snag at her.

"Ethan?" she called.

The chilled air held no reply. Branches snapped to her left and her hand went to her gun. She backed against a tree trunk, heart pounding, until she caught Titus's bark. Blowing out a breath, she followed the sound. Slipping on the debris, she lost them for a moment until she heard another shout from Ethan to her right.

She scooted down a hillock, mostly on her bottom due to the thick layer of wet leaves. In a crevice sheltered by a cluster of tall pines, she found Ethan standing over yet another pile of rocks. Ethan's expression was unreadable. To her horror, she saw Titus lying down, staring intently at Ethan, a posture that said everything.

Surely it could not be. Her eyes must be deceiving her. Titus must be confused about his new training. "That isn't…"

Ethan bent slightly, as if he'd been punched in the gut. "He beelined right here, no question about it. Circled three times and lay down, just like I trained him."

He crouched by the dog, absently praising him and rubbing his ears. "I...I think he alerted earlier. Remember when we were training before with the fake scent? But I pulled him off to go help Mindy after she fell off her bike." He grimaced. "I should have let him do his thing then. He was trying to do his job and I got in his way."

The moan of the wind accelerated, driving rain into her face with stinging lashes. She forced the question out. "So there's another body?"

The shock rippled across his face. "Yes," he said. "A second one."

Cold forced its way down deep inside her, past the disbelief. "Ethan, what is going on here? We know it wasn't Andy, and it couldn't have been Sullivan. Who has been killing people and burying them in the woods?"

"Right behind Jillian's house," he finished.

She stared at him. It had not occurred to her. Two bodies buried virtually in Jillian's backyard.

"Get her on the phone, will you?" Ethan said, standing. "I want to talk to her before the police come calling."

She thought as she dialed, *What could Jillian possibly know about two dead bodies?*

In his office, Colonel Masters paced in front of his wall of photos, Ethan, Titus and Kendra squeezed into the corner chairs.

"Why do you have to bring that hound in here?" Masters snapped.

"K-9 training, Sir. We're a team, all the time, not just when we're at Canyon."

Masters appeared too agitated to note the smile on Ethan's face, so Ethan sent Kendra a sly wink. She didn't exactly smile, but he thought she might have relaxed a fraction.

Jillian joined them and this time he did not feel a jolt at the sight of her. But he did notice the worry lines carved around her mouth.

"These bodies," she said, hands on hips. "I can't believe it. Right behind my house."

"Two women," Ethan said, "and according to the coroner's unofficial findings, buried within days or weeks of each other."

"I've got more unofficial intel," Masters barked. "The first body you found looks to be a twenty-year-old female named Elizabeth Carver. She was a local, worked at a bar across town called Oasis."

"How'd they get the ID so quickly?" Kendra asked.

"She was buried along with her purse and wallet. And some money and gold jewelry, so the motive wasn't robbery. She didn't show up for work about eight months ago, but the bartender assumed she skipped out. No family came looking or filed a report. As I said, this is all unofficial until the coroner does a complete analysis, but it's probably Elizabeth Carver." He looked at Jillian. "That name mean anything to you?"

Jillian folded her arms. "No, and in answer to your next question, I'm not a 'hang out in a bar' kind of woman. I've never been to Oasis. I mean, since I started renting that house two years ago, I've barely been home at all. When I'm not deployed, I'm training and when I'm not training..." She shrugged.

You have plenty of other places to stay, Ethan thought ruefully.

"The other body is also a female of similar age. No ID so that's going to take longer. These are complications, slowing our progress." Masters glowered at Ethan and Kendra. "You two. What have you accomplished on the Sullivan case?"

Ethan related their findings about Lara Dennis. "We're also looking again at the list of prison visitors." He did not care to share specifics about the Chase McLear investigation. Until he had evidence on the guy besides a name suddenly appearing where it hadn't been, he wasn't going to smear McLear's reputation.

"So in other words, you have nothing, only some vague idea that he's got a female accomplice but no further proof about whom. And now," Masters said, his face purpling as he looked at Kendra, "you've brought in another complication. Andy Bleakman and your twisted love life."

As Kendra tensed beside him, Ethan stood. "Don't talk to her like that. She didn't bring anyone in. Bleakman tracked her here after he was released from prison."

"I know the details," Masters snapped, "because I ran them down, since neither of you bothered to brief me. Kendra, I've half a mind to fire you."

Kendra stood and gazed calmly at Masters, though Ethan saw her cheeks blossom with color. "If that is what you feel is best, go ahead. I am still going to continue tracking Sullivan until Jillian is safe whether I'm employed by you or not."

"With a stalker at your heels?" Masters asked.

"I will deal with that, too."

The colonel's nostrils flared. "Bleakman is your problem and these bodies are the cops' burden to handle. All I care about is Sullivan. He, or his accomplice, has taken a couple of whacks at killing you, so we're close."

Ethan's hands fisted at the cavalier way he tossed Kendra's safety around, but Kendra only smiled.

"There's a sunny point," she said, and he could not help but chuckle at her droll humor. What spirit she had.

"But we need to speed things up, force his hand," Masters continued.

Ethan's gut tightened. "How?"

"I've made some calls. Jillian's going to deploy to Afghanistan."

Ethan shot a look at Jillian. She did not show surprise. "You okay with that?"

She brushed the hair from her eyes. "Yeah. I think it's for the best. You know how I love the rush."

He did, but he also knew she did not like the feeling that she was running away from a threat. It wasn't in her makeup. Then again, noting the uncertainty he saw in her eyes, perhaps she was changing.

Maybe he was, too. He found that though he'd never love her again, he could hope good things for her. "When do you leave?"

"This afternoon," Jillian said. "Vans depart at sixteen hundred hours for Fort Levine, where we get final briefings."

Ethan remembered an earlier conversation. "So you're flying out with Bill Madding's unit?"

Her face sparked some emotion. "Yes, but I told you. We're over."

Ethan waited for the rush of anger or suspicion, but it did not come. "Good," Ethan found himself saying. "You can do better than Madding."

Her mouth quirked in surprise. "Thanks."

Masters continued, "We'll make Jillian's deployment very public. Sullivan will want to take her out here before she leaves the base so you'll be standing in, Kendra. Jillian will secretly take an earlier flight to Fort Levine, right after she leaves this meeting." He handed Kendra a garment bag. "Here's your flight suit and a duffel so you look the part. You're dismissed."

Jillian followed them into the hallway. "I don't like to be leaving it like this. Be careful, you two."

"We will," Kendra nodded, hugging her.

Ethan shook her hand. "Watch your back, Lieutenant."

"I will. And you do the same." Her mouth crimped in thought. "You two make a good team," she said. "Better than we ever did, Ethan."

There was no malice there, no caustic undertone to the remark. He accepted it with a semi-puzzled nod.

She walked down the hallway without a backward glance.

Ethan touched Kendra on the shoulder as they walked to his truck. "You don't have to do this. You can quit."

She fired a plucky smile. "What? And miss the exciting finale?"

"Figured you'd had enough excitement to last you a lifetime."

"To be honest, I think you're right, but I made a promise and I'm going to see it through."

"Duty to Masters?"

"No, to Jillian."

"She doesn't realize what kind of a friend she has in you."

"No matter what she's done, she saved my life. Besides, I think she's changed just a bit, don't you?"

Ethan took a deep breath. "Yes, and maybe I have, too."

"Not drinking your own poison?"

He knew it was true, finally. *Thank You, God. And thank you, Kendra.* She'd given him the gift of listening, understanding and a loyal friendship he'd never known with a woman before. "Yes, ma'am," he said, awed. "I believe you might be correct."

"Aren't I always?" she said, poking him with an elbow.

"You're beginning to sound like me."

She put on her best Southern accent. "Then let's get busy, partner."

With a massive eye roll, he led the way outside.

TWENTY-ONE

Kendra felt even more like an impostor in her flight suit when they reported to the assigned area on the base. The number of people crowding around the assembled military vans made her nervous. Wives stood close to their husbands, cradling children. Girlfriends clung to their young pilots, trying to keep from crying. Though no one said it, they all felt the dangerous reality of deploying to a war zone.

But at the moment, civilian life was a deadly game as well.

Kendra thought about the two twentysomethings buried and forgotten in the woods. Had they dated marines? Likely, in a town set smack up next to Baylor. Her heart throbbed thinking of the people who would mourn them when they were officially identified. So many lives destroyed and they hadn't a single clue as to why. No answers, only more and more questions.

Ethan touched her hand. "You all right?"

She nodded. "Head in the game, right?"

He glanced at the gathering. "Best case would be to spot and apprehend Sullivan before he makes his move."

Everyone within her line of sight had the appropriate visitor tags on, or base identification. But Boyd Sullivan had his own ID, acquired from the marine he'd murdered. In spite of the heightened security, with a uniform and an ID he could probably sneak into a lot of places on base without a second look.

Ethan's expression was pleasant, but his eyes were intense, scanning everyone who got close, Titus tethered to him by a short lead. Ethan was in ABUs, no rifle, only a handgun tucked under his top, since he was supposed to be playing the part of her soon-to-be spouse, an airman on a Marine Corps base.

A couple strolled by, the uniformed man's arm wrapped around the woman's waist, murmuring something into her ear that made her giggle.

Ethan suddenly pulled her into an embrace that sent her heart racing.

"What are you doing?" she gasped.

His chin grazed her neck. "Preparing to miss you when you deploy," he said. "We gotta blend. Awesome acting. It's one of my skills."

But the kiss he brushed over her neck and temple did not feel like the work of an actor. *Oh, stop it, Kendra. He's pretending, remember that.*

Still, the kisses kicked up her pulse and sparked a ridiculous longing that she could be his partner, his confidante, his woman. If things were different…if she was not a dead ringer for his ex, if Andy was not a permanent threat hovering over her, if he was not too soured on marriage…

Head in the game, she reprimanded herself.

Ethan scrutinized the crowd from over her shoulder and she tried to do the same, but his proximity made the task difficult. Finally he let her ease out of his arms and she recovered enough to study someone she'd noticed in passing.

Behind the refreshment table covered by a dark linen tablecloth, a marine tended to the coffeepot. There was nothing outwardly different about him and she wondered why he'd caught her attention.

Kendra listened with half an ear to the talk around her.

...when you come back.

...I'll miss you so much.

...email every day if you can.

She noticed Bill Madding approach. She tensed as the pilot, who had accosted her outside the gas station believing she was Jillian, looked closely at her, forcing her back a step. "Another impersonation gig? You're more in demand than Elvis."

"Keep your voice down," Ethan snapped.

Madding huffed. "Don't give me orders."

Ethan shot him a forced smile. "I'm doing my job. Why don't you focus on doing yours? Fly your plane, protect your country and stay away from Jillian."

"The real one?" His eyes darkened. "We're deploying together. How is my behavior with her any of your business? You're not back together with her for real."

"Because I don't want to see any woman get mixed up with a low-down snake like you."

Anger flashed over Madding's face. For a moment, Kendra thought he was going to let loose with a punch, but instead he scowled and walked away.

She blew out a breath. "I wonder what Jillian ever saw in him."

"All ego and limited charm, which doesn't speak well to her tastes." He sighed. "Of course, she chose me, too, so…"

Kendra's attention again drifted to the marine fiddling with the coffeepot. He had dark blond hair, a small mouth and his lips were thinned in concentration, but there was something about him… His posture, the way he looked out of the corner of his eye every so often, the sheen of perspiration on his brow. "Ethan?"

"Yeah?"

She saw the guy reflected in the silver surface of the coffee machine, a dark shadow followed by a glint of metal, as he pulled a weapon from under his shirt. "Gun," she shouted, going for her own.

The man at the coffeepot turned and aimed his weapon at her, center mass. It was as if time stood still and at long last she was face-to-face with Boyd Sullivan. Both Ethan and Titus charged at the same moment, leaping between Kendra and Sullivan. The roar of a shot cut across her senses as Sullivan fired. Ethan jerked back a step.

Sullivan overturned the coffee cart, sending a river of hot liquid and mugs crashing to the ground. Soldiers scrambled after Sullivan, civilians pushed children behind them and ran for the safety of buildings. Someone near her shouted into a radio.

Sullivan raced around the end of the last military van. She bolted after him, catching up as he edged around the van. Bringing her gun up, she turned the corner of the vehicle and plunged in, finding herself looking down the barrel of his gun.

"Drop your weapon, Sullivan," she said.

"I was just about to say the same thing."

Kendra noted a shadow creeping over the hood of the van. A marine, gun drawn, was inching closer.

"It's over," she said. "You won't get out of here alive."

"You'd be surprised what I can do," he said. As he fingered the trigger, she braced herself and aimed for his heart, just as the marine edged closer. Sullivan caught the movement, fired one shot at the marine and a second at her. Both shots missed. She wheeled back behind the van. Risking a quick look, she bent down and saw the marine searching under the vans, a furious look on his face and her heart sank when he did not find his quarry. They'd lost him. Again.

She got to her feet.

And suddenly, there Sullivan was, across the quad. He aimed a mocking salute at her.

She did not have a clear shot and he knew it. "There," Kendra shouted, alerting the marine and his cohorts.

Sullivan's smile was tight and filled with hate as he disappeared into the darkness, the marines shouting orders hot on his trail.

His smugness baffled her. He could not possibly escape this time, not from a Marine Corps base. Then her brain processed the shot, Ethan's reaction as Sullivan's bullet caught him. *No. It can't be...*

Fear pumping her legs, she ran.

Ethan was already getting to his feet, blood darkening the shoulder of his fatigues where the bullet had grazed his bicep. Titus stayed close by, whining, but this time he let Kendra in.

"Are you...?"

"Oh, yeah," he said. "Just a nick. I told you Sullivan couldn't hit the broad side of a barn."

She was crushed by both relief and frustration. "I almost had him, but he got away again."

"Marines will get him." Ethan grimaced as he grabbed Titus's lead. "I'll help. Titus can track him."

She stilled him with a hand on his arm. "No, you're going to see the doctor."

"But I'm—"

"Not going to argue, just like the time you plopped me on the stretcher and wouldn't listen to a single world I said."

"That was different."

"Why? And if you say 'because you're a girl' you'll get a sock in the jaw, bullet wound or no."

He was spared from answering when two Marine medics hustled over to assist. They gave Titus a wary look.

"Sorry, guys," Ethan said. "If you want me, you get him, too."

Grumbling, they checked Ethan's vitals, applied a bandage and loaded him into a vehicle with Titus in the back. Another vehicle pulled up and the driver motioned for Kendra. Before she left him, Ethan handed her his pack and phone. "Can you hold on to these for me? Don't wanna bleed on them." He quirked an eyebrow at her. "It's okay. We messed up Sullivan's plans. He didn't hurt you. He might even give up, since Jillian…I mean, since you're going away for seven months."

She took comfort in that. At least for now, Jillian Masters was safe. But she'd never be completely in the clear until Sullivan was captured. It still felt as though she'd failed. All she could do was hope and pray that the marines would track him down and make sure Ethan would get proper medical treatment in spite of his stubbornness.

After a quick drive, she sat as patiently as she could at the base hospital waiting room, checking in with Officer Carpenter by phone. "Do you have anything further on the two bodies in the woods?"

"I told you I'd let you know when we had more info. You can't rush our coroner, and believe me, I've tried," Carpenter said.

She was going to press harder when she felt Ethan's phone vibrate in her pocket. She fished it out in time to see the message appear on the screen.

G.I. Joe. I'm driving to your girl's house. Tell her to come out or I'm coming in to get her. No cops, or things will get bloody.

Adrenaline exploded in her veins. Andy was waiting, laying a trap for Ethan in order to get to her. She'd had her showdown with Sullivan.

Now it was time for another, and this one was personal.

Ethan endured the wound cleaning and the obligatory patient care instructions. He stopped listening to the doctor when Hector Sanchez pushed into the room.

"Give us a minute, Doc?" Hector said.

"You can have all the minutes you want," the doctor said. "He's free to go."

When they were alone, Hector sat heavily in a vinyl-covered chair.

Ethan's heart sank. "You didn't get him."

"No, we didn't."

Ethan slammed a palm on the exam table. "How is that possible? How could Sullivan get away from your security guys on a fenced Marine Corps base?"

Hector huffed. "We think he may have climbed underneath a fuel truck leaving through the gate."

"And your people didn't check?"

"They did, but they must have missed him."

"Titus wouldn't have."

Hector exhaled and glared right back at Ethan. "Yeah? Well, we didn't have Titus on duty, now did we, hotshot? And you didn't fill me in on the 'let's trap Sullivan' plan so I was going in blind, wasn't I? You tied my hands and I don't appreciate it."

Ethan ground his teeth together. It wasn't the time for

blame. They hadn't done any better at Canyon. "Right. Sorry."

Hector sighed. "We found his stolen Marine uniform a mile away from the base. He's not getting back onto Baylor that way."

"My guess is he's not planning on returning at all since as far as he knows his target is going overseas for seven months."

"You sure about that?"

"Let's call it a hunch," Ethan said. "Sullivan has plenty of other targets on his list and he's not a particularly patient man. He can't afford to be with the US Marines and Air Force hunting him. If he wants to get his kills in, he knows he's gonna have to make his moves elsewhere."

Hector let that sink in, and Ethan could almost see the wheels turning.

"What is it you want to ask, Hector?"

"Jillian Masters, or the girl whose impersonating her." He sat up straighter. "What about her?"

"If she's supposed to be pretending to deploy with her squadron, why did my guys tell me that she checked out the front gate?"

He froze. "When?"

"'Bout fifteen minutes ago."

He reached for his phone, groaning when he remembered. Kendra had it, and for some reason, she'd made the insane decision to leave base without him.

He could think of only one reason she might have done that. One very deadly reason.

TWENTY-TWO

Kendra thanked the driver for giving her a ride when he dropped her at the curb a block from her house. She stood in the shadows of some dripping oak trees. Andy's text to Ethan was a trap, of course, one she could not let Ethan walk into. And he would, willingly, delivering himself to Andy to save her. He would believe he could win, but no one won against Andy Bleakman. Until now.

There was no option but for her to face Andy before Ethan did. If it was not now, it would be another day, another place, but it would come, their showdown. She would do her best to win, to end it, finally, but at least she would know that Ethan had not been devoured by Andy's voracious need for revenge. Hopefully the whole nightmare would be over and done with before Ethan was discharged from the clinic.

Her throat was dry, her hands ice-cold as she observed the house. A strange car was parked in Jillian's driveway. Another one Andy had stolen, probably. She took a picture and texted it to Carpenter, whom she had already called. He would be arriving in ten minutes, no lights, no sirens. Her job would be to draw Andy out and he would be arrested. Clean and neat. But nothing with Andy was ever clean, nor neat.

She'd taken a moment before she left Baylor to change into jeans, a T-shirt and a windbreaker, taking the 9mm Beretta from Jillian's survival vest and stowing it in a holster she'd strapped on her ankle, one round chambered, safety off. She'd rather have had her Glock strapped to her side, but he would detect that in a moment. The Beretta would do and she prayed she wouldn't have to use it.

A cold drizzle fell steadily, dampening her hair. Just over the top of the fence she saw the light shining in Ethan's unit behind the house. Andy knew Ethan would not deliver Kendra. He intended to get Ethan and Titus out of the picture first. What surprise had he prepared in the mother-in-law unit? The house? Was he right now crouching behind a curtain with a gun in hand?

She remembered the sound of the wasps swarming over her, the pain of their stingers plunging into her skin, the whir of bullets whistling over her head and the crash of her car hitting a tree. And her headlong hurtle into the icy waters of the river.

Andy's text replayed in her mind. *You're dead.*

Fear suddenly turned to anger that such a man could have power over her life and Ethan's. Yes, she'd made mistakes, craved love too much, trusted blindly and stupidly, but God had saved her from her grievous errors. He'd forgiven her, allowed her to move on, to experience what a decent man was like. More than decent.

Her heart beat the truth with every pulse. She loved Ethan. He'd become the light in her darkness, the God-loving, joke-cracking embodiment of what a man, a real man, a partner, should be like. But he was not open for a relationship, not now, and not with her. As much as it hurt, she knew it was reality. Shoving the pain down, she wiped rain and tears from her face and straightened. If all she could do was ensure Ethan's safety by handling things with Andy, so be it. It would be her gift to him and to herself.

There was no movement from the house, nor the mother-in-law unit. She checked her watch. Another five minutes max until Carpenter arrived.

Baby, she thought suddenly, her stomach clenching into a fist. If Andy had gotten into the main house, what would he do to Baby? She thought of the time long ago when he'd tried to kill the cat, the fury in his eyes, the desire to maim, to inflict maximum pain. Panic nearly forced her feet into motion.

Calm down, she ordered herself. Baby was an expert at hiding and she didn't like Andy one bit. The first sign of him and she'd have scooted to the nearest hidey-hole. *It's fine. Baby is okay and you're not going to do something dumb like go in there without backup.*

A car approached and she tensed, ready to take cover. Mindy Zeppler rolled down her window. "Jillian? What in the world are you doing standing there in the rain? I almost didn't see you."

"I, uh, I just needed some air."

"I heard in town this morning that you were deploying, but you didn't say anything about it to me." There was a flash of hurt in her eyes, betrayal.

"I'm going to catch a ride to Fort Levine later, but yes, I'm deploying." And there'd be no need to continue to impersonate Jillian Masters, no need to stay in this part of Texas. No reason to be around Ethan. She swallowed. "It came up suddenly. I'm sorry I didn't tell you."

Mindy shrugged. "That's the military for you. My ex deploys today, too, but he never minded the short notice. Billy was always chomping at the bit to leave home."

How sad. Kendra felt in that moment that if God

blessed her with a spouse, a home, she'd never, ever want to leave it.

"But aren't you sad to be leaving your hubby?" Mindy asked her. "What about the wedding?"

Kendra forced a smile. "We'll have that beach wedding when I get back."

"Ethan's a good man to wait for you."

"Yes, he is," she said.

"Do you need a ride somewhere? You're getting soaked."

"No." Kendra felt desperate to get Mindy safely away before the cops arrived and the situation went critical. "No, I'm just going to, um, drive to the corner store and buy more cat food. I'll see you later."

Before Mindy could question her, Kendra jogged across the street to her car and slid into the driver's seat. She watched with a sigh of relief as Mindy drove by with a bemused smile and a wave.

The woman thought she was crazy, but at least she would be safely inside before anything happened. Kendra checked her watch again. It was time. Where were the cops?

An arm wrapped around her throat from the back seat.

"I figured you might get in sooner or later. Patience is a virtue, isn't it, Kendra?" Andy said into her ear.

Ethan borrowed a phone and slammed the SUV into gear. Titus braced himself in the back. They flew off the base and along the road toward Jillian's house. His nerves screamed with tension, louder than they had in a combat zone. On the fourth ring Carpenter finally answered his phone.

"I'm en route there right now," he said when Ethan told him to meet at Jillian's house. "Just pulling up on the street."

"It's a trap," Ethan practically shouted. "Andy figured I'd show up and he'd take me and Titus out first. He's in position already, I know it."

"Not my first rodeo, kid," Carpenter growled. "Let us handle securing the scene. You stand down, do you hear me?"

"Yes, sir," Ethan said, ending the connection with a stab of his finger. But hearing and listening were two different things, as Kendra said. He practically throttled the steering wheel, picturing her taking off without him to handle Andy, the psycho. What was she thinking?

But he knew. She'd told him.

I made the mess. I have to clean it up.

Her determination alternately awakened his admiration and his flat-out exasperation. She was actually planning to face down Andy Bleakman alone in order to keep him out of the picture. It was ludicrous. He careened down the highway and the thought floored him. He'd never been with a woman who put his needs ahead of hers. It was stunning, breathtaking and utterly infuriating. He pressed the accelerator harder and nearly missed the turn to her street, pulling up a block away behind Carpenter's car. Fear knotted his stomach when he noticed that Kendra's car was missing. The MP in him imagined the scenario. Kendra had surprised Andy. He'd rendered her unconscious, or worse, and taken her car to escape. Or he'd forced her into the vehicle and taken her somewhere.

Fear accelerated his breathing. *Work the scene*, he told himself savagely.

"I told you to stand down," Carpenter barked, a radio in one hand, as he and Titus hurtled from the truck. "I've got an APB out on her vehicle. My people are inside checking."

"Titus can check faster." He didn't wait for an answer,

clipping Titus to the leash and pulling his sidearm. "Tell your cops I'm coming in."

"You're gonna get yourself killed."

"Tell them," he snapped.

Carpenter relayed the message. "I ordered them all to the yard. Clear the house and if you find him, don't be a hero."

Ethan didn't answer as he and Titus ran to the front door and pushed their way inside.

Kendra drove slowly, her mind searching for escape possibilities. Andy kept a firm hold on her throat, his nails cutting into her skin, and a handgun at her temple.

"Cozy, huh? Our reunion? Just the two of us without G.I. Joe and his dog."

"You don't want to do this," she said.

"Oh, yes, I do. I really, really do." His breath was hot and sour on her cheek. "You betrayed me and I got sent to prison while you went off and had your jolly life as a PI. That's why you're playing at being G.I. Jane, isn't it? Undercover work? Made it harder to find you, but I'm a good investigator, too."

She battled back the fear. "They'll come after you. They know you ducked your parole."

"That's my problem to deal with, but judging from the level of cop expertise around here, I'll be fine. You called them, I assume. They're probably out in front of your house now. They'll look for your car soon, but they won't find it in time."

In time.

"They'll be busy for a while, cleaning up the mess."

Her heart stopped. "What mess?"

He laughed. "G.I. Joe's going to have an accident."

"No," she said, twisting. He pressed the gun harder until it ground against her skull.

"Drive the car," he grated out through clenched teeth.

Tears of pain and fear blurred her vision as she drove slowly around the block. There were no houses along the stretch, just a cement-covered culvert that funneled water back out to the river and the woods beyond.

"Here," he said. "Turn here."

"There's no road. I can't—"

He tightened his hold and she coughed.

"Drive over the culvert, Kendra."

No, her mind screamed.

"We're going to take a walk in the woods, just you and me."

"I won't do it," she whispered.

His fingernails sliced into her neck. "You will do what I want," he said as he squeezed harder, "or I'll knock you out, but that wouldn't be as much fun."

Hardly able to breathe, she guided the car over the culvert and onto a flat section of ground that paralleled the back of the fenced properties. Why didn't he want them to drive away from the house? To put some distance between him and the police? Fingers clutching the wheel, she kept the car creeping forward until he commanded her to stop.

He peered past her at the fence next to the car. A fresh eruption of goose bumps swallowed her up as she realized they were parked behind Jillian Masters's property.

"Do you know who killed those girls, Andy?"

"What girls?"

He would give away nothing and she would never know the truth.

"This is the perfect spot," he said. "Park the car."

With quaking hands she turned off the engine.

Andy laughed. "So easy. One quick stop at the hardware store. Cell phone, pressure cooker bomb, little camera to let me know when they make entry. Too easy."

A bomb. Her mind struggled to process the information. It could not be true. He was bluffing. "Andy, no," she started.

Not loosening his grip, he kicked open the door and dragged her from the car, walking her to the nearest tree.

"Sit," he ordered.

"I don't want to."

With a kick he swiped the legs out from under her and she collapsed to the wet pine needles, falling onto her knees.

"You've got to watch this, Kendra."

He shoved the cell phone in front of her face. "Would you look at that? G.I. Joe has just pushed the door open. Let's see what happens next."

She saw Ethan there on the screen, crouched low, Titus nosing forward past him through the hallway, checking for intruders, looking for her. Everything inside her screamed in terror. "No," she said. "No, please don't, Andy. Please."

Andy just smiled, madness glinting in his eyes. "Watch, Kendra. You won't want to miss a minute."

Ethan's face, raised to the camera, was grainy, indistinct, but her mind filled in the fine details, eyes tender and filled with humor, strong shoulders that had helped carry her burdens, a heart that beat for others.

"Please," she said to Andy one more time. "Hurt me, don't hurt him."

"Oh, I will, Kendra. Don't worry about that." He stepped back and pulled the phone away from her. She bent into a tight ball, her fingers finding the gun in her ankle holster. Her skin was slick with sweat, hands trembling. One shot, one chance. In one fluid movement she stood and drew her weapon.

"Stop, Andy."

He tipped his head back and laughed. Her finger pulled the trigger as his tapped the cell phone.

Ethan kept low as they breached the door of the mother-in-law unit. Titus did not alert on any intruders but still he kept the dog close. Andy wouldn't hesitate to target the dog. The lights were on in the small kitchen, and he cleared the small place quickly. Nothing. So sign that Andy had ever been there.

Final stop was the kitchen. That was where his eyes latched onto the device on the counter.

Pressure cooker bomb.

Adrenaline flashed through him.

He grabbed Titus and hurtled for the back door, ripping it open as the bomb exploded. He felt a massive force of air pick them both up, heard a sound that detonated inside his head with such percussive force that everything went quiet. As if in slow motion, he saw himself tumbling over and over, blown into the wet yard, saw Titus landing several feet to his right. Still.

TWENTY-THREE

Kendra realized the scream that split the air was her own. There were voices, shouts from behind her that she finally understood came from Jillian's backyard. On limbs that refused to cooperate, she scrambled to Andy, who was sprawled backward on the ground, and kicked the cell phone away from where he'd dropped it, pocketing his gun. His eyes were closed, blood staining his windbreaker. With fingers that seemed to belong to someone else, she checked his neck for a pulse.

A tiny beat thrummed. He was alive. Her bullet had caught him right of center, missing his heart. His eyes flicked open and he stared at her.

"Didn't think you'd have the guts, Kendra."

She was too frantic to answer, too crazed to get to Ethan, yet terrified of what she'd find. The gate opened and Officer Carpenter ran toward her with another officer, both with weapons drawn.

"Andy Bleakman?" he asked, eyes on the moaning man.

She nodded.

"Ambulance is rolling."

"Thanks," Andy said, his mouth pulled into a grimace. "Nice to know I'll be well cared for."

"Oh, we don't care much at all," Carpenter said. "We just want you well enough to stand trial so we can send you to prison for good this time."

Kendra was staring at the gate, willing her legs to carry her into the yard so she could see. She had to see. But her body would simply not respond to the commands of her brain. Legs gone rubbery, she could only stand there, gaping, fearing, mourning, afraid to know, afraid to not.

The seconds ticked by. She looked at Carpenter, her expression somber.

"Is…?" she started, then stopped when she caught movement out of the corner of her eye.

Ethan stumbled through the gate, his eyes latching on hers and then flicking to Andy on the ground. Blood dripped from his forehead and his expression was dazed. Nerves firing and spirit soaring, she ran to him and he crushed her in an embrace. He pressed a kiss to her mouth that brought praises welling into her soul, a comfort so sweet she thought she might die of it. Then he wrapped her in a tight hug that smelled of smoke and sweat and she clung to him.

"Ethan," she murmured. "Ethan, I love you. I love you so much."

He did not react, simply squeezed her tighter. Then he seemed to sag and she pulled away. "Ethan?"

He watched her mouth and pointed to his ear. "I can't hear."

The explosion. He hadn't heard her profession of love, not one word.

"I…" She was going to repeat it, but instead she touched her fingers to his face, to his trembling mouth.

Tears welled in the brown depths, grief that robbed the light from his eyes. Grief for…?

She jolted as she realized Titus was not with them.

"Oh, Ethan…" The lump in her throat squeezed off the sound.

His head sagged, his forehead pressed to hers.

"No, no," she whispered.

He heaved in a ragged breath, pressed close for one final moment, then turned and limped back into the yard. Heart pounding, she followed. The backyard was abuzz with activity. A fire engine had arrived, pouring water through the broken front window of the mother-in-law unit, where a small fire licked at the kitchen curtains. Three police officers were directing neighbors away. Kendra saw Mindy in the distance, offering a tentative wave, her face white as paper in the darkness.

Kendra could not lift her hand to return the gesture.

An officer beckoned Ethan, who knelt next to a dark heap on the grass. Titus. *No*, her mind screamed. *God, please let it not be Titus.*

But it was and the dog did not move, even when Ethan knelt over him, cradling the still form as if it was a child. His shoulders were shaking, and then he stood quickly when the cop finished his radio message.

"We're ready," the cop informed him. "We called your people at the number you gave us and asked them to meet us at the nearest animal hospital. I've got you a ride out front."

Ethan couldn't hear and the officer gestured toward the squad car that awaited. Tears streaming down his face, he lifted Titus in his arms and turned one anguished look at Kendra.

"I'm sorry," she said. "I'm so sorry."

She knew he could not hear her as he turned and carried his dog out of the yard.

* * *

Hours later, Kendra could not sleep. There had been no word from Ethan about Titus's condition and she suspected the worst. Her heart broke a little with each passing moment. What had she done to him? What had she cost him by bringing Andy into his world like some horrible pestilence? Worst of all, she'd thought she could handle it herself, deal with Andy alone, and her arrogance had seemingly cost the life of a noble animal, Ethan's closest friend. Her arrogance, like Jillian's, had cut him down.

She remembered how Ethan and Titus had hunted for Baby, scoured the bushes and shrubs for hours to rescue a bony cat for a stranger, and one who was impersonating his ex-wife to boot. They'd come so many miles since then, sharing little bits of themselves, the slivers of pain and joy and mistakes and triumphs, and best of all, laughter. She smiled through her tears thinking about his wild story about marrying her on the beach.

Just a story, but sweet enough to last her for a lifetime. She would try to see him once more, to say goodbye and thank you and… How could she express the terrible regret she felt at what she now expected had happened to Titus? She'd have to try before she left town. She owed him that at least. The doorbell chimed. Ethan? Heart soaring she ran to the door and threw it open.

Mindy stood there holding a container of soup, startled. "I…um… It seemed like a good time for soup."

Kendra sighed. "You're very kind. Thank you." She stood aside to let Mindy into the kitchen.

She set the container on the counter. "What happened, Jillian? The police said there was an explosion, but they wouldn't tell why."

"Someone set a bomb in the mother-in-law unit."

Her eyes rounded. "Who would do that?"

"The ex-boyfriend I told you about."

Mindy shook her head. "What did you do to upset him that much?"

Kendra kept her flare of temper in check. "Mindy, it's late and I'm not going to get into it. He's in custody, that's all that matters."

"Is Ethan okay?"

"Yes, but Titus…" She swallowed hard. "He's at the vet with him."

"Oh." Mindy shoved her hands into her pockets. "You must feel terrible."

"I do. The bomb could have killed them both."

"I meant, how you've treated Ethan."

"How I've…?" She'd almost forgotten. She was Jillian, not Kendra. She could go ahead and explain it, but until she was officially dismissed by the colonel, she was still Jillian Masters, and she owned her friend's mistakes as well as her own. "I'm tired, Mindy."

She ignored the remark. "I mean you cheated on him. Repeatedly." A bright sheen crept into her eyes. "And he took you back, even though you didn't deserve it, and now you've cost him his dog. I hope he doesn't forgive you for that."

Kendra jerked back. "I know you were hurt, Mindy, but you don't have the right—"

"Sure I do," she said. "My husband cheated on me with two other women, you see. He wasn't just sleeping with you."

Her mouth fell open. "Your ex is…"

"Billy Madding, the man you're going to deploy with." She glared. "Isn't that nice? You'll have all the time in the world to rekindle your tawdry affair."

"Mindy, this isn't what you think."

"No? That's what the other two said before they died."

Chills erupted along Kendra's spine. "The other two?"

Mindy cocked her head. "Elizabeth and Jackie. The two young bimbos he was having affairs with. I killed them," she said. "And buried them in the woods."

Jillian's words came back to her.

I dumped him when I saw the text on his cell phone from someone named Lizzie with all the kissing emojis. Lizzie... Elizabeth. The truth crashed home with a vengeance. The woman accomplice wasn't an accomplice at all. They'd been so focused on the trees they hadn't seen the forest.

"That's why I moved to this house, next to you, with the woods behind. It's taken a long time to work it all out." She sighed. "Titus almost ruined everything prematurely when he sniffed out one of the bodies a few days ago, but I pretended to see a stranger and rode down into the creek, threw the binoculars under a shrub. Clever, huh? It worked so well. You two were completely freaked. Totally distracted you from the bodies."

"Mindy..."

"It was a matter of time until Titus found the dead girls, of course, but I was having trouble getting close to you. Shooting your tires out would have put anyone else out of commission, but not you. No, not you. The wasps were fun, but that was pure theater. Running you down after your wilderness survival drill didn't work, either."

"All those attempts, they were your doing, to punish me?" Not Sullivan? Not Andy? Her brain struggled to process it all.

"Surprised, aren't you? Who would expect the mousy neighbor? So easy to ignore. Billy certainly ignored me on a regular basis. Well, I'm not as dumb as you all think I am. I made those girls pay for cheating with Billy. I buried them deep, but you know what?" She stepped closer. "I left a spot for you." Madness, like in Andy, like in Sullivan, shone in Mindy bright as a neon sign.

"I'm not Jillian," she blurted. "My name is…"

"Nice try," Mindy said, cutting her off.

Kendra fumbled for the drawer behind her. If she could get a knife, a rolling pin, something to defend herself…

Mindy took a Taser from her pocket and fired.

Kendra's scream was locked inside as ribbons of fire coursed through her and she fell to the floor.

Bleary-eyed, Kendra swam back to consciousness. Images of Andy, an explosion, Ethan's tears, jumbled through her mind as she gradually resurfaced. It took her several moments to figure out that she was in the driver's seat of Mindy's car, the same car that had nearly run her down on the bridge, parked in Jillian's garage. Her wrists were duct-taped together around the bottom of the steering wheel and there was another strip of tape across her mouth. Her whole body pulsed with one message…terror.

"You're a bad person," Mindy was saying matter-of-factly. "I mean, you have a stalker ex-boyfriend trying to kill you, and me. Plus I heard rumors that you're a target of this Red Rose Killer who the air force is hunting. Three people want you dead. That should tell you something right there."

Kendra tried to flex her wrists, breathing hard through her nose.

Mindy leaned in the open window. "I had an even better idea than burying you in the woods, one that will draw less attention from the cops," she said with a girlish giggle. "Here's how it goes. You borrowed my car, see, since yours was impounded for evidence, and unbeknownst to me, you were so overcome with remorse about being such a tawdry home wrecker and killing Ethan's dog, that you decided to kill yourself. Tragic, huh?" She patted Kendra's hand.

Kendra recoiled from the touch.

"Don't worry. After you're dead, I'll take off the duct tape so it looks real official and I'll be sure to tell Ethan that you were so sorry for treating him like you did so he will think you had a shred of remorse. That will help him heal. He'll be better off without you. So much better."

She reached over and started the ignition. "'Night, Jillian."

Kendra fought the panic. It could not end like this. She'd hurt Ethan in the most grievous way, taking away Titus because she'd insisted on doing things on her own... like Jillian, she thought. And worse, he would take responsibility in his heart that he had not seen through Mindy. Kendra had destroyed Ethan Webb and he hadn't even heard her say she loved him. Maybe that was kinder. Despair darkened her vision.

She slammed back and forth against the seat, trying to loosen the duct tape, begging Mindy with her eyes.

Don't do this. Please.

Mindy leaned close. "You don't deserve a future with a good man like him. Think about that while you die."

Kendra screamed through the tape as Mindy let herself out the side garage door and closed it behind her.

TWENTY-FOUR

Ethan still felt as if he'd been run over by a Humvee, but at least the roar in his ears had subsided to a dull ringing. He paced the floor of the local emergency room where they'd all but forced him after he'd taken Titus to the closest animal hospital. They didn't have to tell him how close he'd come to death. He knew. A second more and he would have been killed and if Kendra hadn't been able to draw her gun in time...

A chill gripped him, the kind that gets you after the battle has been fought, when the full impact comes home to roost on your psyche. But she was alive. His vision blurred as he thought of the other victim, Titus. Dogs could not talk, of course, but Titus had told him in so many ways, "I would give my life for yours without hesitation." There was no greater love than that. He'd been blessed, pure and simple. *Please, Lord, let Titus make it.* Swallowing hard, he texted Kendra again in spite of the late hour.

She didn't answer. Again. Something niggled deep down in his gut.

Was she sleeping?

He should leave her alone to rest, but he burned to talk to her, to hear her voice if only for a moment. The explosion had changed him somehow, though he didn't fully understand how. It was as if the blast had bulldozed away the stubborn barriers he'd constructed to keep him from his own happiness. The past regrets, fears, had vanished and in their place was one echoing desire overriding his senses. *Find Kendra and make her yours, no matter what it takes.*

He dialed again.

The phone rang and rang before it went to voice mail.

The niggle of unease expanded to a quiver.

He texted again and called.

Maybe she doesn't want to talk to you. The thought stopped him. He'd given her enough reasons to cut him out by pushing her away, comparing her to Jillian, hanging on to his own failings. Besides, she had her life back. Andy was in custody and her role as Jillian had come to an end. Maybe she'd packed up and gone. Still, she would have said goodbye, wouldn't she?

Unless he'd misjudged her.

Misread feelings.

Believed she felt affection for him when it was really only circumstantial need. Like his ex-wife.

Doubt. He'd let it in and now he felt paralyzed by it. He looked at the screen again and felt a twitch that sent him pacing afresh. Facts and emotions twirled themselves together but one thread kept coming to the top.

The bodies in the woods. They did not fit in either investigation. It wasn't Andy, and it wasn't Sullivan. The coroner said both women were likely stabbed in the back, not especially deep thrusts, but deep enough to kill. It made him think the perpetrator wasn't a man.

Then there was the proximity of the graves to Jillian's house. With acres of woods, why choose somewhere so close, where discovery would be much more likely? The location was a message of some sort, by someone who hated Jillian, perhaps. Someone who could go in and out of the woods without being noticed.

He picked up the phone and called Officer Carpenter.

"Stop yelling," Carpenter said.

"Sorry, my ears are still ringing. Did you find any connection between those victims in the woods?"

"No connection to each other, but we did some interviews with some frequent fliers at the bar. Got one interesting tidbit."

"Yeah?"

"Both women were seen drinking at Oasis, and both with a local guy."

"Who?"

"Captain Bill Madding. Trouble is, he was out of the area at training around the time the coroner figures the first victim was killed. We're looking into his family connections. There's an ex-wife." An ex-wife. Ethan suddenly remembered a moment from their visit to Mindy Zeppler's house. *I guess it's harder for me to let go than it was for Billy. He'll never be lonely. Women swarm to combat pilots...* All Ethan's suspicions cleared up in his mind, and he knew. His heart slammed into his ribs. "It's not Madding," he said. "It's Mindy Zeppler."

Carpenter frowned and looked at his notebook. "We've turned up nothing substantial on her yet."

"It's her. Madding cheated on her repeatedly. She discovered he was having an affair with Jillian and those other women." He forced the words over his dry tongue. "Kendra's not answering her phone or texts."

"I'm rolling now. We'll take care of it. Stay—"

Ethan didn't wait for the cop's orders. He was already pulling on his dirty ABUs, tossing the hospital clothes on the floor. He raced past the startled nurse and the security guard at the door.

As he sprinted into the parking lot, he felt keenly the absence of Titus by his side. This mission he would have to complete alone. Once in the truck, he sped to Jillian's house, praying with each twist and turn that he would not be too late. His pulse hammered home the truth.

Kendra was everything he longed for. Everything he needed. He was a better man when she was with him and he wasn't going to lose her.

Yanking the truck to the curb and hurtling from the car, Ethan ran straight to Kendra's front door, pounding hard and yelling her name. Carpenter rolled up a moment later.

Ethan slammed his palm on the wood again. "No response."

"I'll check the rear door," Carpenter said.

Then Ethan heard it, a soft low rumble, the sound of an engine.

"The garage." The main door was closed and he did not know the code to override it. The gate to the yard was locked. He took a running start and climbed over, splinters sinking deep into his flesh, his breath raging in his lungs. He made it over the gate and landed hard on the other side, scrambling to his feet and throwing himself at the side door to the garage. He flung it open, and his senses were assaulted by the smell of car exhaust. Slamming a hand on the garage button, he opened the big door, releasing the cloud of noxious carbon monoxide that had built up in the enclosed space. He ran to the driver's side, nerves on fire as he saw Kendra slumped behind the wheel.

"Kendra, I'm here, I'm here," he shouted. Was he too late? No, he would not allow his mind to think so. He cut the ignition, pulled a knife from his pocket and began to saw her wrists free of the duct tape. He thought he noticed her eyes flicker open, a slit, only a crack that ignited a firestorm of hope in him.

"I'll get you outside to some fresh air. You're gonna be okay."

Her eyes widened a crack more and he saw the warning spark in them.

He whirled just in time to avoid Mindy Zeppler's stun gun. She stumbled against the car, losing her grip on the weapon, and he snaked a boot around her ankle, sending her to the floor where she thrashed and screamed.

Carpenter sprinted up, quickly turned Mindy on her stomach and pulled her hands behind her back. "Get her out of here," he said, coughing.

Ethan didn't need the direction. He finished slicing through the tape and dragged Kendra from the car, carrying her out onto the grass. Inside the garage, Carpenter was handcuffing Mindy Zeppler.

"Jillian's a tramp, Ethan," she screamed. "She fooled around with Bill, just like those other girls. She deserves to die."

No, he thought, looking into Mindy's hate-filled eyes. No matter what Jillian had done, she didn't deserve to die. And Kendra… She had been hurt many times over, by her family and by a man, just like Mindy, but she'd chosen another way, the only way.

He turned away from Mindy and peeled away the tape from Kendra's mouth as gently as he could. He began chafing her hands. "Come back to me, honey," he said. "I'm right here waiting for you."

He stroked her hair and her face, his fingers tracing the contours of her cheeks, her brows. This woman, his woman, with a broken past and a golden future.

Their future.

"Come back," he whispered, one more time.

An agonizing headache, nausea, confusion. That was all Kendra could identify. She felt as though she was underwater, surfacing only long enough to see the doctor's face and watch Ethan speak words she could not hear, his expression grave. There was a vague sense of time passing, minutes turning into hours. Somehow, she finally emerged from the water, awake enough to discover it was the next morning.

The doctor said she was recovered sufficiently to be discharged from the local hospital. She wasn't sure. Her body was well enough, but her spirit would not lie easy. As the noxious chemicals left her body, she still felt keenly how much she'd cost Ethan, Mindy's words working their way into her flesh like a spiked thorn.

You don't deserve a future with a good man like him.

Maybe Mindy was right. He didn't promise her anything anyway. *He saved your life, isn't that enough?*

But it wasn't, not nearly enough to salve the ache in her soul as she ran through the plans in her mind. Pack up. Reengage in her PI business. On to the next case, the next part of her life without him.

As soon as the doctor finished her discharge papers, she pulled on clothes that somebody had brought for her, Ethan perhaps. Blindly she punched the elevator button and made her way to the parking lot, blinking against the onslaught of sunshine, looking for a cab.

"Going my way?"

She jumped, spotting Ethan's newly repaired truck at the curb, him standing at the passenger side, beckoning. She allowed her feet to carry her to him and he folded her into a hug.

"I step out to get some coffee and come back to find that you've been discharged. How are you feeling?"

"Headachy, but alive."

"Yes, ma'am." He grinned. "I thought we could celebrate your operational status with a little lunch back at my place, if you're up to it. Got something I want to show you."

The brown eyes, so warm, the strong arms, not meant for her, created an unbearable level of pain. "Oh, I'm not sure. I should be packing up, giving my final report to Colonel Masters."

"He can wait," Ethan said. "The investigation team at Canyon needs a face-to-face report anyway, so we might as well knock two things off the to-do list."

How could she resist that smile, the crinkle under his eyes, the almost dimple on his cheek? She must be still groggy from the carbon monoxide, but she found herself unable to do anything but acquiesce. A few more hours, and she meant to savor each precious moment of them. "Okay. I guess packing can wait."

"Yes, ma'am," he said. Once they were in the car, he tuned the radio to the country station as they made the drive back toward Canyon. His fingers drummed a sultry rhythm on the steering wheel and the warmth of the June morning seeped inside her, lulling and comforting her. If only she could stay in the moment, live in it…

To her mortification, she awoke a little while later, just as they were entering the base.

"I slept. I can't believe it. I'm sorry."

"You should be. You missed some amazing music." He stroked her hand. "Anyway, you've been through a lot. You've earned a rest."

"A lot" didn't nearly cover it. She wondered how long it would be before she could rid herself of memories of

Andy and his bomb, Mindy and her Taser. She shivered and he gripped her fingers.

"Allow yourself to feel and remember," he said softly. "And then try to let it go."

Let it go. How would he ever let go of losing Titus? she wondered. She yearned to tell him again that she was sorry, to ease the burden she knew he must be feeling, but the words stuck in her throat, sharp edged like glass.

"Okay to make a stop?" he said.

She nodded. He checked in with security at Canyon and drove to the K-9 training center. Her heart sank as they got out. Was it time to place Ethan with a new dog? Already?

Master Sergeant Westley James poked his head out the front door. "Thought I heard you. Ready? Because he is."

Ethan chuckled. "Might want to stand behind me, Kendra."

The door opened and Kendra's mouth dropped open as Titus shot through the gap, running full tilt at Ethan. The dog slowed only a moment before leaping up and knocking Ethan to the ground. Titus tongued Ethan's face until Ethan pushed him back a piece.

"Oh, all right. I get it. You didn't want me to leave you here, but these docs had to check you out for themselves." Titus finished licking Ethan and raced to Kendra, wriggling his rump and slurping up the tears that dripped from her face.

"I thought...I thought he was..." she mumbled.

"Nah. Titus is stubborn, just like his handler. He's tougher than an overcooked brisket." His face softened. "I told you in the hospital, but you must have been a little fuzzy still."

She laughed and rubbed Titus down until the dog returned to Ethan for some more licking. *He's alive*, she kept saying to herself. *Thank You, God.*

They loaded Titus into the truck and went to Ethan's base apartment. He picked up a wicker picnic basket from the counter. "Not too hot yet. Figured we'd hit the beach."

"What? There's no beach around here."

He waggled his eyebrows. "That is where you are mistaken, Ms. Bell. Come along. Close your eyes please." Laughing, she complied, took his hand and he led her to the backyard, where they stood on the porch, bathed in June warmth.

"All right. Eyes open."

She blinked against the sunlight, as an unbelievable scene came slowly into focus. Sand glittered on top of a big blue tarp, an inflatable palm tree sticking out of the gritty pile. There were a couple of shells tossed onto the sand and a beach ball nearby, which Titus promptly went after, his paws batting it ahead of his snapping teeth.

Ethan had spread a blanket in the middle of the sand and there he placed the picnic basket and handed her a pair of pink sparkly flip-flops.

"Gotta have the proper footwear. I guessed at the size."

Laughing so hard she almost could not breathe, she took off her shoes and put on the flip-flops, while he donned a ridiculous multicolored bucket hat patterned with flamingos.

"Are you feeling all beachy now?" he said, eyebrows wiggling.

She stopped her laughing long enough to answer. "Yes, but you didn't have to go to all this trouble just for me."

His face grew serious. "Yes, I did. We need to start planning."

"Planning what?"

His shoulders rose and fell with the force of a deep breath. "Our wedding."

Wedding. She'd imagined him saying it, surely.

"It's gonna be at the beach, remember?" he said.

Kendra froze. She'd heard wrong. It was her heart overriding her ears. But there he was, sinking down on one knee in the sand, doffing his flamingo print hat as he fished a ring from his front pocket.

"Kendra Bell, I love you. I want you to marry me."

She gaped. "But… I…" She closed her mouth, her throat suddenly too thick to speak, just as her mind was unable to process what she was hearing. *I love you.* It must be her own desire confusing her, tricking her senses.

He took her hand and kissed it. "I love you, and let me tell you that was a God thing considering that you look just like my ex-wife. But I think He arranged all that so I could go face-to-face with myself, what I really believed, about forgiveness and trust. Typical of God to do that kind of thing to a poor unsuspecting clod, isn't it?" He smiled.

"Ethan," she whispered. "I hurt you and Titus. You almost died because of me."

He shook his head. "No. We both almost died because of three twisted individuals, two of whom are already in custody. Now, back to what I was saying…"

"My past is a mess."

He laughed. "Mine, too."

"You don't want children."

"I've been stubborn there, too, but now that I've met you, I've reconsidered. Let's start with a few and see where it goes. I'd say we should cap it at a dozen, for sure." His grin grew even wider.

"But—"

"Kendra, we're going to get married and it's going to last forever. You know how I know that?"

She could only shake her head.

"Because I'm not your number one."

She frowned until he pointed a finger at the sky, his expression both soft and serious. "He is. We have Him and He will join us together and keep us together if we always put Him first. He's the best at sorting out messes, the absolute best."

"Yes, He is," she whispered. He'd kept her alive, taught her what love was supposed to look like, helped her to forgive herself. She brushed a finger over Ethan's cheek. And this man had helped.

"I've never felt this way about anyone," he said. "Not Jillian, or anyone. I want a life with you, every day, month, year and decade that I can get. What do you say, Kendra?"

She fought for composure, to make real with words the love that had revived her soul. "I never thought I'd find a man as amazing as you, Ethan. I love you. I'll always love you, every single day of my life."

He rested his cheek in her open hand for a moment, and she thought she heard his breath catch.

"Then you're saying yes?" he asked as he raised his gaze to her.

She could only nod, more tears trickling down her face.

Ethan slipped the ring on her finger and stood, stroking her hair, soaking in every square inch of her face. Kendra's face, not Jillian's.

"I want to take you to meet my mom," he said. "She's my hero and she's going to absolutely adore you."

"Are you sure?" Kendra felt the twist of doubt. "I've not exactly lived a model life."

"Yes, I'm sure. She's going to pull out her girlie yarn and start knitting you a scarf and trying to feed you at every opportunity."

"I'd love that."

His expression suddenly went serious again. "And I'm not going to stop until Sullivan's behind bars for life."

"I happen to know a good private investigator who will be happy to help you in any way she can."

He gazed at her, his heart brimming over into his eyes, and she saw the love there, pure and gentle, a forever promise nestled deep down.

Then he pulled her close and kissed her. She wrapped her arms around him and kissed him back, the sun embracing them both.

Titus, having succeeded in flattening the beach ball, began to dig, spraying them all over with sand. They held their hands up to shield themselves, laughing.

"'Course, it may be a little tough with our blended family," Ethan said. "Cats and dogs, you know."

She laughed. "I think He'll help us with that, too."

He gathered her close again. "You know it, pumpkin," he said, going in for another kiss.

* * * * *

The hunt for the Red Rose Killer continues.
Look for the next exciting stories in the
MILITARY K-9 UNIT *series:*

MISSION TO PROTECT—Terri Reed,
April 2018
BOUND BY DUTY—Valerie Hansen,
May 2018
TOP SECRET TARGET—Dana Mentink,
June 2018
STANDING FAST—Maggie K. Black,
July 2018
RESCUE OPERATION—Lenora Worth,
August 2018
EXPLOSIVE FORCE—Lynette Eason,
September 2018
BATTLE TESTED—Laura Scott,
October 2018
VALIANT DEFENDER—Shirlee McCoy,
November 2018
MILITARY K-9 UNIT CHRISTMAS—
Valerie Hansen and Laura Scott,
December 2018

Dear Reader,

What a pleasure and an honor to spend time writing about our men and women in the military and their fantastic canine partners. Of course, in order to enhance the suspense, some details were tweaked a bit, but it in no way diminishes the amazing service of the K-9s and their handlers. Mark Twain said, "It's not the size of the dog in the fight, it's the size of the fight in the dog." Titus, along with his real-life counterparts, has plenty of fight, courage and loyalty. Truly they are soldiers of the highest caliber.

In addition to their courage, dogs like Titus in this story have legendary detection skills. As hero Ethan Webb explains about his dog Titus, "You walk into a room and smell chili cooking... a dog walks in and smells each ingredient in the pot."

In this story, Titus, Ethan and Kendra are up to their ears in trouble, attempting to track serial killer Boyd Sullivan and a stalker from Kendra's past. As the threats mount, the three will learn to trust each other, and Kendra and Ethan will have to face their own troubled pasts as they begin to fall in love. I hope you enjoy their journey! I love to hear from my readers. If you'd like to connect with me, you can find me on Facebook, Twitter and Instagram. There is also a physical address on my website at *www.danamentink.com* if you prefer to correspond that way. God bless you, my friend!

Sincerely,
Dana Mentink

Get 4 FREE REWARDS!

We'll send you 2 FREE Books plus 2 FREE Mystery Gifts.

Love Inspired® Suspense books feature Christian characters facing challenges to their faith... and lives.

FREE Value Over $20

SPECIAL EXCERPT FROM

*When Chase McLear is accused of aiding the Red Rose
Killer, can Maisy Lockwood, the daughter of one of
the victims, help him clear his name before they both
become targets?*

Read on for a sneak preview of
STANDING FAST by **Maggie K. Black**,
the next book in the **MILITARY K-9 UNIT** *miniseries,*
available July 2018 from Love Inspired Suspense!

The scream was high-pitched and terrified, sending
Senior Airman Chase McLear shooting straight out of
bed like a bullet from a gun. Furious howls from his K-9
beagle, Queenie, sounded the alarm that danger was near.
Chase's long legs propelled him across the floor. He felt
the muscles in his arms tense for an unknown battle, as the
faces of the brave men and women who'd been viciously
killed by Boyd Sullivan, the notorious Red Rose Killer,
flickered like a slide show through his mind.

Sudden pain shot through his sole as his bare foot
landed hard on one of the wooden building blocks his
daughter, Allie, had left scattered across the floor. He
grabbed the door frame and blinked hard. His three-year-
old daughter was crying out in her sleep from her bedroom
down the hall.

Seemed they were both having nightmares tonight.

He started down the hall toward her, ignoring the stinging pain in his foot.

"No!" His daughter's tiny panicked voice filled the darkened air.

"It's okay, Allie! Everything's going to be okay. Daddy's coming!" He reached her room. There in the gentle glow of a night-light was his daughter's tiny form tossing and turning on top of her blankets. Her eyes were still scrunched tightly in sleep.

A loud crack outside yanked his attention to the window at his right. He leaped to his feet and started for the glass just in time to see the blur of a figure rush away through the bushes. His heart pounded like a war drum in his rib cage as he threw open the window. The screen had been slit with what looked like a knife and peeled back, as if someone had tried to get inside

He closed the window firmly, locking it in place. Then he looked down at Queenie. "Stay here. Protect Allie."

Don't miss
STANDING FAST by Maggie K. Black,
available July 2018 wherever
Love Inspired® Suspense books and ebooks are sold.

www.LoveInspired.com